Alice & Megan Forever

Judi Curtin

Illustrations: Woody Fox

THE O'BRIEN PRESS
DUBLIN

First published 2008 by The O'Brien Press Ltd,
12 Terenure Road East, Rathgar, Dublin 6, Ireland.
Tel: +353 1 4923333; Fax: +353 1 4922777
E-mail: books@obrien.ie
Website: www.obrien.ie
Reprinted 2009, 2012, 2015, 2017.
This edition first published 2015 by The O'Brien Press Ltd.

ISBN: 978-1-84717-690-5

2 4 6 8 7 5 3
17 19 21 20 18

Cover design: Nicola Colton
Illustrations: Woody Fox
Layout and design: The O'Brien Press Ltd
Printed and bound by CPI Group (UK) Ltd, Croydon, CR0 4YY
The paper used in this book is produced using pulp from managed forests

The O'Brien Press receives financial assistance from

JUDI CURTIN grew up in Cork and now lives in Limerick, where she is married with three children. Judi is the author of the bestselling 'Eva' and 'Alice & Megan' series. Her books have been published in German, Portuguese, Finnish, Swedish, Norwegian, Russian, Serbian and Turkish, and in Australia and New Zealand.

The 'Alice & Megan' series

Alice Next Door
Alice Again
Don't Ask Alice
Alice in the Middle
Bonjour Alice
Alice & Megan Forever
Alice to the Rescue
Viva Alice

The 'Eva' Series

Eva's Journey
Eva's Holiday
Leave it to Eva
Eva and the Hidden Diary
Only Eva

Time After Time

See If I Care (with Roisin Meaney)

For Dan, Ellen, Brian and Annie

Warmest thanks to:
My family and friends. Extra thanks to Annie who read the first draft and pointed me in the right direction whenever necessary.
Everyone at The O'Brien Press who has worked so hard to make the 'Alice & Megan' series a success – Brenda, Claire, Emma, Helen, Ivan, Kunak, Michael and Ruth. (Thanks also to all the staff slaving away in the background whom I never get to meet.)
Woody for still more great drawings.
The many bookshops and libraries who have invited me to read from the series. Special mention has to go to Hilary and Jo in Bridge Street Books in Wicklow, who rounded up every child within a five-mile radius, and brought them to listen to me.
The staff and pupils of the many schools who invited me to visit. Special thanks to all the girls from my old school (Eglantine NS in Cork), who gave me a wonderful welcome recently.

Chapter one

I finished brushing my hair, and had a quick look in the mirror. I was straightening my tie when Mum looked around my bedroom door.

She gave one of her long sighs.

'Secondary school isn't a fashion parade, you know, Megan,' she said. 'Remember, you're going to school to learn.'

'You don't understand,' I said.

Mum folded her arms.

'Try me,' she said.

I thought about ignoring her, but she was blocking the door, so there was no way I could escape.

Now it was my turn to sigh.

'It's just … it's just that it's the first day … and the first day is the most important day of all. Everyone will be watching everyone else. I have to look my best. I have to look …'

'… cool?' said Mum.

I nodded.

'If people think I'm a loser on the first day, that will never, ever change, no matter what I do. They'll still think I'm a loser in six years time when I leave the school. It would be a total disaster. My life would be ruined forever.'

'That doesn't sound very fair to me,' said Mum.

I picked up a clip Alice had lent me, and

pinned back my hair.

'It's *not* fair,' I said. 'And that's why I have to make sure that it doesn't happen to me.'

I pulled the clip out of my hair again, and threw it onto the bed.

Nothing seemed right.

Nothing seemed good enough.

This was the most important day of my life and already I was sure that I was going to mess it up.

Mum came over and hugged me.

'You poor thing,' she said.

Then she went over to the bed and picked up the clip. She carefully twisted one side of my hair, and clipped it neatly into place.

I looked in the mirror and smiled. A miracle had happened. Mum had made me look sort of nice.

'Thanks, Mum,' I said.

She smiled back. 'You're welcome. Anything so long as you won't end up being the school loser. Still, I wish you'd let me knit you a school jumper. It would have been much nicer than that shop-bought one. Now you're going to look just like everyone else.'

I sighed again.

Didn't she know that was the whole point?

Didn't she know that I *had* to look like everyone else?

Didn't she know that if I'd worn a hand-knitted jumper, I might as well have gone to school with the word '*loser*' tattooed on my forehead?

This wasn't the time for a row, though.

'The school is *very* strict,' I said. 'Everyone has to have the exact same jumper. Remember, I told you ages ago. It's the rule.'

'It's a stupid rule, if you ask me,' said Mum.

(It wasn't just a stupid rule – it was a stupid rule that I made up especially, as soon as Mum had started talking about hand-knitted jumpers. I was glad she hadn't phoned up the school to complain. If she discovered the truth she would never, ever let me forget it. She'd probably try to knit me a school skirt as a punishment.)

I pulled up the sleeve of my lovely, shop-bought school jumper, and looked at my watch, trying to give Mum a hint, but she didn't seem to notice. She had that dreamy look on her face again.

'Do you know, Megan, I can still remember my first day of secondary school?' she said.

'Did you bring your pet dinosaur?' I asked grinning.

Mum ignored me.

'My mother made me a huge big bundle of cheese sandwiches and packaged them up in the bread wrapper.'

'So you were a loser,' I said. 'I hope it doesn't run in the family.'

Mum smiled.

'No actually, I wasn't a loser. Everyone used bread wrappers for their sandwiches then. There were no fancy lunch-boxes in those days. I remember—'

Just then the doorbell rang.

'That's Alice,' I said. 'Sorry, Mum, but I can't keep her waiting.'

I pushed past Mum and went to open the front door.

Alice was standing there with a huge smile on her face.

'Ready?' she asked.

I nodded. I was too excited to speak.

My little sister Rosie appeared, still in her pyjamas.

'You and Alice look nice,' she said. 'I wish *I* was going to very big school.'

Suddenly I was a bit afraid of the day ahead. Maybe it would be nice to stay at home with Mum and Rosie.

I felt a hand on my shoulder. I turned to see Mum beside me. She hugged me, and gave me a huge sloppy kiss on the cheek.

'Have a lovely day,' she said.

I pulled away.

'I will. Bye, Mum.'

Then I raced down the path before she could embarrass me any more.

'Bye, Sheila,' called Alice as she raced after me.

Mum gave one wave, and then closed the front door.

I turned to Alice, wiping my cheek where

Mum had kissed me.

'Sorry about all that soppy stuff,' I said. 'That was *soooooo* embarrassing.'

Alice shrugged.

'I thought it was kind of sweet. My mum couldn't see me off. She had to catch an early train to Dublin for a meeting.'

Suddenly I felt sorry for moaning. Even though my mum is a total embarrassment, I'm glad she still lives with my dad. Alice's parents don't live together any more, and even though she's kind of getting used to it, I know she'd love a happy family like mine.

* * *

We walked quickly and soon we were passing our old primary school. It wasn't open yet. I gazed over the wall. It looked small and safe. Part of me was afraid of secondary school. Part of me wished that I could be back in my old school, where I'd know what to expect.

I wondered if I could explain this to Alice.

'Are you sorry we're not going in there?' I asked.

Alice gave a big laugh.

'No way,' she said. 'We've left all that behind us.'

She hesitated.

'You're not sorry, are you?'

Suddenly I felt a bit stupid, so I smiled as happily as I could.

'No,' I said. 'Now hurry up, or we'll be late.'

* * *

Soon we were at the gates of our new school. Our best friends, Grace and Louise, were waiting outside for us. We all hugged and jumped up and down a bit.

'Who's excited?' asked Louise.

We all shouted together.

'I am!'

I wasn't really lying. I *was* excited. It's just that I was afraid too.

I gazed up at what was going to be my school for the next six years. It looked bigger and scarier than it had when I'd attended the open day with Mum and Dad.

'Who's a tiny, tiny bit afraid?' said Alice suddenly.

I could feel my face going red.

Was Alice reading my mind again?

Was she picking on me?

Was she trying to make me look stupid in front of the others?

Then Alice slowly put her hand up.

'I'm a bit afraid,' she said.

'Me too,' said Grace and Louise together.

I smiled. Now I didn't feel so bad.

'Me too,' I said.

Then we all had one more hug, and walked quickly into our new school.

Chapter two

We walked through the huge front doors. I looked around. Everything seemed big and strange. There was a strong smell of polish, like someone had been cleaning the place especially for our arrival.

On the wall in front of us was a big

printed sign – *'First Year Students This Way'*. An arrow pointed to the right.

Alice, Grace, Louise and I joined lots more nervous-looking first years as we all made our way down a long corridor.

'Where's everyone else?' asked Alice.

'It's only first years today, remember?' said Louise.

I was glad of that. This place was scary enough as it was.

Another arrow directed us into a big assembly hall. I saw a few boys and girls from my old school, and lots and lots of strangers. Some of the boys were trying to look tough. Most people were chatting nervously. Some stood alone, looking even more scared than I felt. One small, dark-haired girl looked like she was going to cry. I was *soooooo* glad I was with my friends.

'I so hope we're all in the same class,' said

Grace. 'Do you think we might be?'

I don't know why Alice and Louise didn't answer. I didn't answer because this was the thing I'd been worrying about. This was the reason I hadn't been able to sleep properly for the last few nights.

At the open day we'd been told that boys' and girls' names were put into two hats, and classes were drawn at random, with equal amounts of girls and boys in each group. There were four classes. If I didn't get into the same one as Alice, I didn't know what I'd do. Alice said it didn't matter. She said we'd still be best friends no matter what happened. I knew she was probably right, but if she was my best friend, I wanted her right next to me.

I didn't want to be stuck at the other end of the school with a big load of strangers. I wanted to be with Alice. I always wanted to be with Alice.

But what could I do?

It was all down to a draw that had already been made. Somewhere there were four lists of names that could ruin my life forever.

*   *   *

Just then the principal, Mrs Kingston, walked on to the stage, and everyone stopped talking. Mrs Kingston launched into a huge, long, boring speech about how we had to be the best we could be and stuff like that. I couldn't concentrate though. All I could think of was the bundle of white paper that she held in her hand.

After what felt like hundreds of years, Mrs Kingston stopped talking and held the sheets of paper in the air.

Everyone stopped shuffling their feet and fixing their ties. This was the big moment, and we all knew it.

'As you know,' said Mrs Kingston. 'You are going to be divided into four classes. We have done this randomly, as we feel this is the best way.'

Get on with it, I felt like saying.

Didn't she know how awful this was for us?

Didn't she know that this was the *only* thing that mattered?

'Some of you are going to be happy,' continued Mrs Kingston. 'And I'm afraid some of you are going to be disappointed. It is school policy not to change classes once they have been allocated, so please don't ask. If you aren't with your friends, please try not to be too upset. You can still see each other at break times and after school. And of course, this is your big chance to make some new friends.'

But I didn't want new friends. I liked the friends I had already.

Mrs Kingston was smiling again. Easy for her. Her life wasn't in danger of being ruined forever in the next few minutes.

'Anyway,' she said. 'Keep in mind the fact that these classes are only for the first three years. After the Junior Cert you'll all be mixed up again.'

Now I felt like crying.

Who cared about after the Junior Cert?

That was three years away.

I was worried about tomorrow.

And the next day.

And the day after that.

Mrs Kingston was making a big fuss of putting on her glasses. At last she spoke again.

'Class J. When I call your name please join Mr Leavy at door 3 and follow him to your classroom.'

Everyone looked towards door 3 where a kind-looking man was smiling at us.

'I've heard that Mr Leavy is really nice,' whispered Alice. 'I hope we get him.'

I didn't answer. I didn't care what teacher we got. As long as Alice and I were together, I didn't care if we had the meanest teacher in the history of the world.

At last, Mrs Kingston started to call out the names. I felt like I was in kind of a trance. There were only four names that mattered to me – all the rest were just words.

Suddenly Alice poked me in the ribs.

'She said Grace's name. Grace is in class J.'

I didn't answer. I was so nervous, I'd somehow managed not to hear Grace's name being called.

I held my breath.

Most of all I wanted to be with Alice, but it would be nice if Grace and Louise could be with us too.

Was there any chance that all four of us could be together?

After a few more names, Mrs Kingston folded the first sheet of paper, and put it on the table beside her.

'That's it,' she said. 'That's Class J.'

Grace hugged Alice, Louise and me, and headed for door 3. Seconds later, Mr Leavy and his students were gone, and the door was closed behind them. I felt sorry that Grace had to go, but I was glad that it wasn't Alice who was leaving. There was still a chance that we could be together.

Before we could say anything, Mrs Kingston was speaking again.

'Class K,' she said. 'Miss Lynch is waiting for you at the double doors at the end of the hall.'

Immediately she began to call out names.

When she got to the end of the list, she still hadn't called Alice or Louise or me.

'Only two classes left,' whispered Alice. 'That's good news.'

Was it?

I was so worried, I couldn't think straight.

'Class L,' began Mrs Kingston. 'Alice O'Rourke, Kate O'Mahony … …'

I didn't dare to breathe. Every time Mrs Kingston called a name that wasn't mine, I felt a sharp pain in my side, like someone was stabbing me. When she called Louise's name, Louise and Alice hugged each other quickly. Then Alice reached across and squeezed my hand so tightly that it hurt.

Soon Mrs Kingston said, '... and the last person in class L is Megan ……'

I started to smile, and actually gave a little skip of joy before Mrs Kingston finished. '…… Murphy. Now boys and girls, hurry along to door 4 where Miss Falvey is waiting for you.'

It wasn't me. It was another Megan.

Alice and Louise were going to be together, and I was going to be on my own.

I could feel tears at the back of my eyes.

But how could I cry now?

I'd be a loser, and everyone would know it.

Alice was hugging me.

'Come with us, Megan,' she said. 'No one will notice.'

Even though I felt so sad, I had to smile. Only Alice could think of something like that.

'They've got lists,' I said. 'They'll notice if one class has an extra person.'

'I suppose you're right,' said Alice sadly.

Then she gave a sudden smile.

'I know,' she said. 'We'll find that other

Megan, and ask her to swap with you. I'll tell her it's really, really important. I bet she won't mind. And by the time the teachers notice that you've swapped, you'll both be settled in your new classes, and it wouldn't be fair to swap you back. And the teachers won't be cross, because you're both called Megan. They'll just think you didn't hear properly.'

It sounded like a crazy idea, but sometimes Alice's crazy ideas actually work. For a moment, it seemed like a possibility.

Then Louise pulled my arm.

'Look,' she said, pointing across the room. 'That's Megan Murphy – over there with the blue hair-band. I know her from swimming lessons.'

The girl she was pointing at was happily hugging two other girls.

'I'll ask her anyway,' said Alice.

I shook my head.

'Don't bother. She's with her friends. She won't want to swap with me. It's all fixed. Now go with your class, or you'll get into trouble.'

Alice hugged me again.

'Don't worry,' she said. 'You'll be fine.'

I couldn't reply.

I wouldn't be fine.

I wanted to run up to Mrs Kingston, get on my knees and beg her to put me into Alice's class.

I wanted to sit on the floor and cry my eyes out.

I wanted to run home, throw myself into Mum's arms, and forget all about stupid, stupid secondary school.

But I was thirteen.

I was supposed to be all grown up and sensible and brave.

So I tried very hard to smile at Alice and said, 'Sure, I'll be fine.'

I hugged her one more time.

'See you later,' said Alice.

Then she and Louise ran off after their class.

Mrs Kingston had come down from the stage. She looked at the group of us who were left standing around looking at each other.

'You boys and girls who are left are Class M. Please follow me and I'll take you to your classroom where your form tutor Mr Spillane is waiting for you.'

So I pinched myself very hard to make sure I didn't cry and followed my new class out of the assembly hall.

It was half past nine on the most important day of my life, and already I hated secondary school.

Chapter three

Mrs Kingston flung open the door of the classroom.

'Your new students are here, Mr Spillane,' she announced.

Mr Spillane was sitting at the top of the classroom. He looked serious, but not too cross.

'Welcome to secondary school,' he said. 'As it's the first day, you can just sit wherever you like.'

Great.

He'd said the worst words in the world.

The words I had been dreading.

Now everyone in the class would think

that I had no friends.

Friends at the other end of the school weren't much use to me now.

Suddenly I heard a familiar voice.

'Megan, over here!'

I quickly turned around and saw a girl called Jane, who had been in my class at primary school. She was sitting in one of the very front seats. She smiled at me, and patted the chair next to her.

'This seat is free,' she said.

I gulped. This was exactly like when I'd started sixth class, back when Alice was living in Dublin. A whole year had passed, but things were still the same. Jane was still such a loser that she didn't even mind being a loser. I think she actually *liked* being a loser. And if I sat beside her, everyone would think I was a loser too.

So I pretended not to hear her, and

walked the other way.

I know that was really mean of me.

I know I should have felt sorry for Jane.

But I couldn't.

I was too busy feeling sorry for myself.

I looked around desperately. I didn't know any of the other girls in the room. There were a few boys I knew from primary school, but they were all together in a big huddle. One of them looked up and smiled at me. I smiled back, but I knew he wouldn't want me hanging around with him.

I found an empty seat in the middle of the room and sat down. More people came into the classroom. Some looked at me for a second, and then they walked on, as if they'd just decided I wasn't worth sitting next to. Maybe I shouldn't have let Mum clip up my hair. Maybe it looked stupid. I wished I'd asked Alice what she thought. I wished I didn't have to be on my own.

Then, when almost all of the seats were taken, a friendly-looking girl came along.

'Can I sit here?' she asked.

I was afraid to answer – afraid that she was talking to someone else. Then, when no one answered, I tried not to sound too happy.

'Sure,' I said.

'I'm Kellie,' she said as she put her bag on to the desk.

I found myself smiling at her. Maybe this wasn't so hard after all.

'I'm—', I started to say, when there was a shout from the other side of the room.

'Kellie. We're over here. Come and sit with us. We've saved you a place.'

Kellie looked embarrassed.

'Do you mind?' she asked.

Of course I minded.

But what could I say?

I have no other friends?

Please sit down here?

Don't leave me alone?

How sad would that sound?

So I smiled and said, 'That's OK,' like I didn't care one way or the other. Then Kellie picked up her bag and went to sit with her friends.

It looked like everyone had arrived, and the only empty seat was the one next to mine. Mr Spillane was talking to the principal, and everyone else except for me was chatting. At the front of the room, I could see that even Jane had found a friend, a serious-looking girl, just like herself.

I took out my homework diary and pretended to be really interested in reading the study tips on the front page. Then I heard footsteps. I looked up to see a totally cool boy. He was tall and thin, and his long, dark hair had a streak of purple down one side. He was wearing a school jumper and trousers, but his shirt was open at the neck, and he wasn't wearing a tie.

'That seat free?' he said, pointing to the very free seat next to me.

I nodded, not trusting myself to speak.

He sat down, and I got the funny feeling that everyone was staring at him, and at me. Just then the principal left the room, and Mr Spillane asked us all to be quiet.

'You should all have received a copy of the dress code, and I see that most of you have taken it on board.'

Then he pointed to the boy next to me.

'You, young man, what's your name?'

'Marcus,' he muttered.

'Well, Marcus, it seems that your copy of

the school dress code must have got lost in the post. Shirts are to be correctly closed, ties are required at all times, and purple hair simply isn't allowed. Come and see me after class, please.'

'OK,' said Marcus.

I felt sorry for him. Imagine getting into trouble on your very first day.

Then Marcus turned to me and whispered, 'He has *got* to be kidding. I'm expected to take clothes advice from someone wearing a jumper with dolphins on it?'

I giggled, but stopped when I realised that Mr Spillane was staring at me.

I might not have any friends, but at least with Marcus around I had a feeling that our class was going to be interesting.

* * *

It felt like a very long morning. We got long

lectures about keeping our books in order, and about all kinds of school rules. We were shown our lockers and where to put our coats and our sports bags. We were shown the toilets, the lunch rooms, the principal's office and the lost-property room. After a while it started to remind me of the forest in France where Alice and I had got lost last summer; there were so many corridors, and each one looked the same as all the others. I was sure I'd get lost and never be found again.

At last it was twelve o'clock, and we were allowed to go home.

It had been the longest three hours of my life.

* * *

I waited at the school gate for my friends. Grace arrived first, with two other girls.

'Hi, Megan. This is Rebecca and this is

Hannah,' she said. 'Rebecca is in my riding school, and Hannah is her friend. They're both in my class.'

I couldn't help feeling jealous. I had hoped Grace would understand how I felt about being in a class on my own, but already she had two friends. It was looking like I was going to be the only loner in the entire year.

Just then Alice and Louise arrived.

'How did you get on?' asked Alice. 'Have you made any friends yet? Who did you sit beside?'

At least I didn't have to say that I'd sat on my own.

'I sat with a boy called Marcus,' I said casually.

'Marcus? Not Marcus Wall?' asked Louise in a shocked voice.

I shrugged.

'Don't know his second name.'

'Is he skinny, and has he got long hair with purple bits in it?' she continued.

I nodded.

'That's him.'

'And you weren't afraid?'

I looked at her in surprise.

'Why should I be afraid?' I asked.

'Marcus lives on my road,' she said. 'He's *always* in trouble. He's really bad.'

I gulped. Marcus hadn't seemed very scary when he was sitting next to me in class, but now I was starting to wonder if I'd missed something.

Then I noticed something strange. Because of Marcus, everyone had forgotten about me. No one need know that I had no real friends. As long as Marcus was around, maybe no one would guess that I was a loner.

Chapter four

Next morning Alice and I walked to school together again. Once more we passed our old primary school, and once more, part of me wished we could still go there. Part of me even wished I could be inside in my old classroom being bullied by Melissa (the meanest girl from our old class.)

When we got to our new school, I stopped at the front door for a second. I pretended I was tying my shoe-lace, but really I was trying to find the courage to go inside. Now that the older students were back, school seemed even scarier than before. Big boys who looked like men were pushing past me. Tall girls who looked like models were laughing and hugging each other. I felt very small, and very afraid.

When we finally went inside, Alice pointed to the left.

'My locker's this way,' she said. 'Which way is yours?'

I wasn't brave enough to tell her that I couldn't remember. I'd been too confused yesterday by the time we got to our lockers.

Just then I saw Jane and her new best friend walking to the right. I knew their lockers were near mine.

I smiled bravely at Alice.

'My locker's the other way,' I said.

'See you later?' she asked.

I nodded.

'At the canteen?' she said.

I nodded again, hoping that when the time came, I'd actually be able to find the canteen. Then I followed Jane until we got to our lockers.

The corridor with the lockers was crowded, with everyone pushing and shoving and scrambling to get their books ready. I had to find all the books and copies that I needed for the first three classes.

'I'll never get the hang of this,' I muttered to myself.

Jane leaned over and smiled.

'Don't worry,' she said. 'The first few days

will be hard for all of us. After that, it'll be fine.'

That made me feel a bit better, but then I felt bad for what had happened yesterday. Jane might be a loser, but at least she was a loser who was being nice to me.

At last I had my books ready, and I followed Jane and her new best friend to our first class, Geography with Mr Spillane.

Most people were there already, and I was faced with the same decisions as the day before. Jane sat with her friend, the boys from primary school sat together and Kellie was with her friends. I sat on my own again.

The class had been going on for ten minutes when Marcus arrived. I was relieved to see that his shirt was buttoned, he was wearing a tie, and there was no sign of purple hair.

'Nice of you to join us,' said Mr Spillane, as Marcus came and sat next to me. 'And I'm happy to see that you've decided to abide by our dress code.'

Marcus didn't answer him, but as soon as Mr Spillane turned to the blackboard, Marcus leaned over towards me. He lifted a lock of his long hair to show me that the purple hair wasn't gone, it was just tucked out of sight under the rest of his hair.

'Take my advice,' he whispered. 'Never let dolphin-man tell you what to do.'

I didn't answer.

Maybe Louise was right. Maybe I should be afraid of Marcus. Still, if I didn't sit next to him, who was I going to sit next to?

* * *

We had to change rooms after every class. That meant picking up everything we owned, and fighting our way through crowds of big people who all seemed to want to go in different directions. Marcus usually vanished during these journeys, and then showed up late to class. Sometimes he smelled of cigarettes.

I quickly decided that the only sensible thing to do was to follow Jane. She seemed to have some special kind of radar that stopped her from ever getting lost. Before long, she noticed that I was always one step behind her, but she didn't seem to mind. Sometimes she even turned around and smiled at me, and I smiled back, glad to see a friendly face.

Once again, it seemed like a very long morning. At lunch-time, I met Alice, Grace and Louise. They all looked happy, but then I decided that maybe they were only pretending, just like me.

‘I love this place,’ said Alice. ‘But I wish it wasn’t so big.’

‘Yeah,’ said Grace. ‘And I wish we didn’t have to carry so many books around at once.’

‘Yeah,’ said Louise. ‘I wish we could just stay in one room, like we used to in primary. I keep forgetting where I’m meant to be, and what books I’m supposed to have.’

‘I wish the classes weren’t so long,’ said Alice. ‘We had double Business Studies today, and it was totally boring.’

‘I wish …,’ I began, and then I stopped. What was the point of wishing for stupid stuff about books and classes?

All I really wished was that I had a friend in my class.

And how could I say that out loud?

Chapter five

The week dragged on. Marcus sat next to me most days. He had hardly any books, so whenever we needed a book, he leaned over and looked into mine. I didn't mind, which was just as well, because I wouldn't have known how to say 'no' to him.

'You sit next to Marcus every day?' said

Alice in surprise when I told her.

I shrugged.

'Why not?'

'What do you talk about?'

'It's class time. We're not supposed to be talking.'

Alice punched me lightly on the arm.

'Stop being such a swot. Honestly! What do you talk about?'

I had to think.

'We don't talk very much.'

'So what do you do?'

Again I had to think.

'I do my work, and mostly Marcus just sits there looking bored, and saying smart stuff about the teachers when they're not looking.'

'That's totally weird.'

Maybe she was right.

'I don't know,' I said. 'It's not like he

wants to be my friend or anything. I don't think he wants to be anyone's friend. I think he just doesn't want to be there.'

'Louise says he hangs out with older boys after school,' said Alice.

'That's it then,' I said. 'He doesn't need friends. He's got enough already. Now, is your French teacher a total pain? Mine is. She makes us repeat stuff over and over again like we're babies.'

Alice laughed and started to tell me a funny story about her French teacher.

I smiled to myself. I was getting good at changing the subject. Alice still had no idea how lonely I felt every morning when she left me to go to her own class.

* * *

Every day when I came home from school, Mum made me sit at the kitchen table.

Every day she made me have a glass of milk.

'You need it for healthy bones,' she said.

Every day she gave me a home-made biscuit that tasted like sawdust.

'Full of fibre,' she said.

Every day she sat down opposite me and said, 'So how are things going at school?'

Every day I wished she was the kind of mum who didn't care anyway – the kind of mum who'd have been perfectly happy with '*fine*' as an answer.

She wasn't that kind of mum though, so mostly I just told her lies.

Then one afternoon, I found I couldn't lie any more. It was all getting too much for me, and I had to talk to someone.

So when Mum said, 'How are things going at school?'

I said, 'Awful. I hate my class.'

Mum looked cross.

'Who are they? Who's being mean to you? Are you being bullied? Do I need to go in and talk to someone about this?'

I shook my head.

'No one's being mean. In a way I wish they were. It's just that I have no one to be friends with. I feel like no one notices me. I say good-bye to Alice in the morning and I don't really talk to anyone else until I meet her and Grace and Louise at lunch-time.'

Mum looked like she was going to cry. I sighed. Maybe telling her hadn't been such a good idea after all.

'So do you sit on your own?'

I shook my head.

'No. Mostly I sit next to a boy called Marcus.'

'A boy?' repeated Mum.

Poor Mum was worried just because he

was a boy. What would she have said if she knew he was a boy with purple hair, who didn't seem to own any school books, and who smoked between classes?

I was beginning to regret getting into this whole conversation.

'It's OK,' I said. 'It's still the first week. I'm sure I'll make some friends soon.'

Mum jumped up.

'That's not good enough,' she said. 'I can see that you're upset, and I don't like that.'

She checked her watch.

'It's only a quarter past four. I'm sure the principal's still at school. Why don't I go over and have a chat with her? I'm sure she could move you to a different class.'

I shook my head sadly.

'That won't work,' I said. 'She told us on the first day that no one's allowed to change. She won't change the rules just for me. You'd only be wasting your time.'

And if you tell the principal, the only thing that will change is that she and all the other teachers will know that I'm a loser.

And then something strange happened. Mum went very quiet. That never happens. Mum *always* has something to say. And for the rest of that evening, she looked like she was watching me, and trying to make up her mind about something.

Chapter six

In the morning, I hadn't time to worry about Mum's strange behaviour any more. I had to figure out how to get to PE on time, and then get changed back into my uniform for class, and have books ready for Science and History and Maths, and do all this without getting lost.

The whole day passed in a blur of fumbling for my keys, and opening and closing my locker. Once I closed the locker door so quickly that I caught my finger inside. It hurt so badly I thought I'd chopped my finger off. I sucked my finger trying to make the pain stop. Tears came to my eyes, but I wiped them away quickly. Everyone was rushing past me, and no one stopped to see if I was OK. No one seemed to care.

I decided to tell Alice about it later, but when I saw her, she wanted to tell me about her Maths teacher, and suddenly the story of my sore finger seemed a bit stupid.

By the time I got home that evening, I had a terrible headache. I felt like there was an alien jumping around inside my skull, stamping his feet and trying to get out.

When I got into the kitchen, there was a box in the middle of the table. It was wrapped up in newspaper, with a piece of old tin foil crumpled up on the top in what was probably meant to be the shape of a bow. Years of living with Mum told me that this was her idea of a present.

'Who's that for?' I asked, wondering who I should be feeling sorry for.

Mum smiled.

'It's for you.'

'But why?'

My mum is *so* not the kind of mum who buys presents when it's not your birthday or Christmas.

She smiled again.

'Dad and I had a talk last night, and we decided to get you a present. It's kind of a starting secondary school present.'

This was very, very strange.

I picked up the box.

'Can I open it?'

Mum shook her head.

'No. Leave it until later. Dad wants to

see you open it.'

'Why? Did he help you knit it?'

Mum looked kind of hurt.

'It's not something knitted,' she said.

'Sorry,' I said, and I actually meant it.

I put the box down on the windowsill. It was nice of them to buy me something, but years of experience had taught me not to get too excited about Mum's presents. It was probably a new dictionary, or a packet of broccoli seeds or something exciting like that. Maybe it was a book – *How to Make Friends When Everyone Thinks You Are a Loser.* I could think of loads of things that could be in the box, but none of them was anything I actually wanted to own.

By the time Dad came home, I had forgotten all about the present. We were sitting down eating our tea, when I heard a strange beeping sound.

'What's that noise?' I said.

'I don't hear anything,' said Mum and Dad together.

'It's a mobile phone,' said Rosie.

'Yeah right,' I said. 'Like anyone in this family has a—'

I stopped talking.

Why were Mum and Dad smiling like that?

Why were they looking over at the newspaper-wrapped box on the window-sill?

And why was the beeping sound getting louder?

Could they …?

Would they …?

Rosie got up from her chair. She went over and picked up the box, and held it to her ear.

'I think there's a phone in here,' she said.

I looked at Mum and Dad. Now they were both smiling so much they looked like their faces were going to burst open.

'Megan, I think you'd better open that box and put us all out of our misery,' said Dad.

I was so excited, my hands were shaking. I ripped off the newspaper, opened the box and found a beautiful, red mobile phone inside. It wasn't a fancy camera phone or a video phone or one that could store a thousand songs, but I didn't care. It was a phone, and it looked like it was mine!

And it was still ringing.

I pressed the green button and held the phone to my ear.

'Hello?' I said.

'Answer quicker the next time or I won't bother calling you any more.'

'Alice?'

She laughed.

'Got it in one.'

'But how ...... what .... ?'

She laughed again.

'Your mum told my mum all about your new phone this morning. She told her the number, and said I was to ring you at tea-time. So that's what I'm doing.'

This was *so* fantastic. I couldn't talk properly because I was so excited.

'Can I call you back later?' I asked.

'Sure,' said Alice. 'You can call me any time, now that you've got a phone!'

I hung up and raced over and hugged Mum and Dad until they begged for mercy. Then I hugged Rosie just because I felt so happy. I sat at the table again, holding my phone, and turning it over in my hand. Just the feel of it was totally great.

'Thank you so, so, so much,' I said.

'You're welcome,' said Mum and Dad together.

Nobody said anything else for a while, but there was something I had to know.

'Why... ' I began, not really sure how to complete the sentence.

Mum and Dad looked at each other.

'You know we don't really approve of mobile phones for girls your age,' said Mum. 'In fact, we think they're quite a bad idea.'

I gulped.

What was she saying?

Had they changed their minds?

How cruel would it be to give me a phone, and then decide it wasn't such a good idea after all?

Could they really take it away after only three and a half minutes?

I slipped my phone into my pocket.

Dad saw me and laughed.

'Don't worry,' he said. 'It's all yours now. We're not going to take it back.'

'We don't approve of phones,' repeated Mum, 'but we don't want you to be different to everyone else.'

Suddenly I began to understand. This was all because I told Mum I had no friends in my class. Mum and Dad thought I'd find it easier to make friends if I had a phone.

Didn't they know it was nothing to do with phones?

Didn't they know it's because I'm not like Alice?

Didn't they know it's because I'm not brave enough to go up to strangers and talk to them?

Because I just sit there quietly and no one notices me?

But I didn't tell Mum and Dad how wrong

they were. They would have been upset, but nothing would have changed. So I gave them another big hug each, and then I sat down and finished my tea.

*   *   *

Later on, Alice called over with a small package wrapped up in pink tissue paper.

'Getting your first phone is a big deal,' she said. 'So I thought I'd better buy you something to mark the occasion.'

I had to smile. Alice was probably on about her fifth phone by now. I pulled the tissue paper off my present, and saw that it was a cute little phone charm in the shape of a teddy.

'It's beautiful,' I said, and Alice looked pleased.

She showed me how to attach it to my phone, and then we sat on my bed and I texted my friends, and felt at last like a normal person.

Chapter seven

Soon it was Monday again. We had assembly first thing, so everyone went in to the huge assembly hall. I stood next to Alice, Grace and Louise.

Could it only have been a week since we'd been standing there on our first day?

It felt like about a hundred years had passed since then.

Mrs Kingston went on and on about loads of boring stuff. Then everyone was given a page with a list of optional subjects on it.

'You can choose one of these subjects,' Mrs Kingston said. 'Take the list home and discuss it with your parents. You must return the sheet tomorrow, with your choice clearly marked. And please try to be mature about your choices. Choose something you would like to study. Don't just pick so you can be with your friends.'

I could feel myself going red.

Could Mrs Kingston see right through my head?

Was she reading my mind?

Anyway, I didn't care what Mrs Kingston said. I was doing the same subject as Alice, even if she picked something I totally hated.

* * *

At lunch-time, the four of us discussed it.

'I'm picking music,' said Louise. 'It's my favourite, and anyway, Mum and Dad said I have to.'

'What about you, Megan?' asked Grace.

I didn't answer at first. I knew it would sound stupid if I said I was going to copy Alice. So I shrugged, like I hadn't really thought about it.

'Not sure yet,' I said.

'I can't make up my mind between Home Economics and Spanish,' said Grace. 'I'd like to do Home Ec, but Spanish would be handy when we go to Lanzarote.'

'I'm definitely doing Home Economics,' said Alice. 'Not poisoning people when they come to visit would be handy.'

We all laughed, and then the bell rang and we had to go back to class.

*　　*　　*

That evening I showed Mum the sheet.

'I'm going to choose Home Economics,' I said quickly, before she even had time to read it properly.

'But I can teach you all you need to know about Home Economics,' she said. 'Why not pick something else? What about Art? Art is a lovely subject.'

I shook my head.

'I *really* want to do Home Ec,' I said, and for once in her life, Mum didn't argue.

* * *

In the end, Alice, Grace and I all decided to do Home Ec. Our first class was on Wednesday.

'For the practical part of this subject, you have to work in groups of three,' said Miss Leonard, our teacher.

I grinned at Grace and Alice, as we all

went to sit together.

It was *so* nice to have friends.

It was *so* nice not being the class loner.

Most of what Miss Leonard said was stuff I knew already, but I didn't care. I was with my friends again, and nothing else mattered.

At the end of the class, Miss Leonard handed out a list of ingredients.

'We have a practical lesson on Friday,' she said. 'You take turns to cook. One person out of each group has to bring in these ingredients. That person will cook, with the other two acting as assistants. This week we're going to make queen cakes.'

For the first time I wondered if I'd picked the right subject. I'd been able to make queen cakes since I was about seven.

Grace looked at Alice and me.

'Who wants to bring in the stuff?' she said.

Alice picked up the page.

'Do you mind if I go first?' she asked. 'I think I might need the most practice.'

Grace and I laughed.

'Whatever!' we said together as Alice carefully folded the list and put it into her schoolbag.

Chapter eight

Home Ec was last class on Friday. I was very glad to get there. Marcus hadn't been at school that day, and even though part of me was a bit relieved, I'd had to sit on my own for every class, and I hated it.

Alice was already in the Home Ec room when Grace and I got there. She had her apron on, and was busy setting out her ingredients on the table. She looked very pleased with herself.

'I've got every single thing ready,' she

said. 'I can't wait to get started. I've got a funny feeling that I'm going to be good at this.'

Miss Leonard clapped her hands.

'Quiet please, everyone,' she said. 'As it's your first week, I've picked something nice and easy. As you saw on the lists I gave you, you just need four ingredients – butter, sugar, eggs and self-raising flour. So now please set those ingredients out on the table in front of you. I'll come around to see how you're getting on.'

'Er ... Alice ...' I began, but just then Miss Leonard came over. She looked at the ingredients lined up on the table in front of Alice. Then she looked at Alice. Alice smiled happily back at her.

'What's your name?' asked Miss Leonard.

'Alice O'Rourke,' said Alice, still smiling.

'Tell me, Alice O'Rourke, is this your idea

of a joke?' said Miss Leonard.

Alice stopped smiling. She looked at Miss Leonard in surprise. Alice is good at jokes, but I could see that for once she was being totally serious.

'No, Miss,' she said.

Grace and I looked at each other. Grace started to smile, but stopped when she saw Miss Leonard's face.

'Read out your ingredient list,' said Miss Leonard.

Alice obediently picked up the list and began to read.

'125 grammes of butter.'

She stopped reading and pointed at the table.

'Look, Miss, I brought butter, and all that other stuff too.'

Miss Leonard didn't look any happier.

'That most certainly is *not* butter. That is

dairy spread,' she said. 'It's completely different to butter, and it certainly isn't suitable for making cakes. And what on earth is this?' As she spoke she held up a small white plastic container.

'That's sugar,' said Alice cheerfully. 'Well, sugar substitute actually. My mum puts it in her coffee. We didn't have any of the other kind. My mum thought this would do. She said—'

Miss Leonard held up her hand to stop Alice talking.

'I don't think we really need to know what your mum said. Now what exactly are *these?*'

She was pointing to two small, speckled, round things. I'd been kind of wondering what they were too.

'They're eggs,' said Alice, but she didn't sound quite as cheerful as before. 'Quails' eggs.'

'QUAILS' EGGS?' repeated Miss Leonard so loudly that everyone else stopped what they were doing and stared over at us.

'Aren't they totally cute?' said Alice. 'It's nearly a pity to break them, isn't it?'

Miss Leonard seemed lost for words, so Alice continued.

'They were on special offer at the supermarket. I thought they'd give an exotic touch to the queen cakes.'

Miss Leonard looked like she was going to explode.

'Alice O'Rourke, this is Home Economics,' she said. 'We don't *do* exotic here. If you want exotic, maybe you should switch to Spanish, or Art or … I don't know. Just something … anything that's not Home Economics.'

I gasped.

What would I do if Alice gave up Home Ec?

Luckily, it's not that easy to get rid of Alice.

'Thanks, Miss,' she said. 'But I like Home Ec. I think I'll stay here, if it's all the same to you.'

I could see that it wasn't all the same to Miss Leonard, but I expect that there are rules about what teachers can say to pupils, and I think that what Miss Leonard wanted to say to Alice would have broken a few of those rules. So she didn't reply.

Alice held up the last ingredient. Miss Leonard examined the clear plastic bag.

'Please say that's flour,' she said weakly. 'Not talcum powder or salt or magic fairy-dust or something else completely inappropriate.'

Alice smiled happily.

'It *is* flour,' she said. 'Real flour, and I weighed it out myself at home. 125

grammes, just like it said on the list.'

Miss Leonard didn't look very impressed.

'See if someone can lend you the other ingredients, and then follow my instructions *very* carefully.'

'Yes, Miss,' said Alice, as Miss Leonard walked away shaking her head.

I giggled.

'That was kind of funny,' I said.

Alice made a face.

'It's easy for you,' she said. 'Your mum could bake cakes in her sleep. My mum couldn't bake a cake to save her life.'

Grace laughed.

'Don't worry,' she said. 'You've got Megan and me to help you.'

Alice shook her head.

'Thanks, but no thanks. How will I learn if I don't try this on my own? You two can sit back and watch. You might learn something.'

Grace and I looked at each other. It was looking like we were going to have a fun afternoon.

Chapter nine

Grace and I learned lots of things that afternoon – lots of thing about how not to make queen cakes.

First Alice turned on the electric mixer at full speed, and sent the butter and sugar she'd borrowed flying into the air. Some of it rained down on Miss Leonard's head. She looked up at the ceiling and shook her head.

'Don't tell me that ceiling is leaking again,' she said. 'I thought that had been repaired during the summer.'

Grace and I had to hide under the table, we were laughing so much. Alice dragged us out.

'Go and borrow more ingredients from someone,' she said crossly. 'I'm just getting the hang of this.'

Grace and I did as she asked, but things only got worse from there. Alice managed to drop one egg on the floor, and then she cracked another one so hard that it slithered out of her hand and all over the table top like a gross, slimy, yellow river. Grace distracted Miss Leonard while Alice cleaned it up, and I tried to find someone else with two eggs to spare.

'Thanks, Meg. Thanks, Grace,' said Alice. 'I'll share the cakes with you both for being so nice.'

'Must you?' asked Grace, and even Alice

laughed at that.

Much, much later, it was time to take the cakes out of the oven.

'Stand back, girls,' said Alice, as she picked up the oven gloves and opened the oven. 'This is my big moment.'

Then she went very quiet. She carried the tray of cakes to our table, and put them down. Miss Leonard came over.

'Those cakes are a total disaster,' she said.

Even Alice couldn't deny that. All the other groups had managed to produce beautiful, golden cakes. Alice's were completely flat and yellow-looking, a bit like stodgy flying-saucers.

Luckily someone at the other side of the room dropped something and Miss Leonard went over to investigate.

'Was that self-raising flour you used?' I asked.

Alice shrugged.

'How would I know? I thought there was only one kind. Anyway it's too late now. Help me pack up and we can get out of here before Miss Leonard finds something else to give out about.'

She shoved the cakes into her bag, gave the table a quick wipe, and then we set off for home.

After a while, a dog started to follow us.

'Look,' said Alice. 'He smells the cakes. The poor little thing must be hungry. Here, doggie. You can have one.'

She reached in to her bag and pulled out a cake. She held it towards the dog. He sniffed carefully, and then ran away whining.

Grace and I laughed.

'What?' said Alice, like she didn't know what was so funny.

Grace and I laughed some more.

Alice shrugged.

'It's not my fault,' she said. 'If there was a class in ordering pizzas, I'd get an A for sure.'

I laughed again. That afternoon had been the most fun I'd had in ages.

Secondary school wasn't turning out the way I had hoped, but I knew I'd always have Home Ec on Fridays to look forward to, and things seemed a little bit better

Chapter ten

On Monday morning, I went to my locker, gathered up my books and walked slowly to my first class. Kellie came in just as I was taking out my homework. She smiled when she saw me.

'Hi, Megan,' she said.

'Hi,' I said back.

I so badly wanted her to sit next to me, but didn't know how to say this without sounding like an idiot. I just hoped that somehow she'd know.

She stood next to my desk for a minute. I

didn't know what to say, and it looked like she didn't either. I thought about telling her about my new phone. Maybe if she knew I had a phone, she'd think I was cool enough to be friends with. But then I changed my mind. Maybe she'd somehow figure out that it was my first phone ever. Or maybe when she heard my phone wasn't a fancy one that could show videos, she'd think I was a total loser.

I tried to think what Alice would do in this situation. I didn't have to think for very long. She'd just ask Kellie to sit down next to her. Suddenly I understood something – if I wanted to make friends in this class, I'd just have to be brave.

I took a deep breath,

'Er, … Kellie …', I began, but before I could finish, Marcus was beside us. He edged past Kellie, and sat in the seat beside me.

'Hi,' he muttered, and then he put his head down on the desk like he was going to go to sleep.

'You were saying?' said Kellie.

I shook my head.

'It's nothing,' I said. 'See you later.'

Kellie shrugged and went to sit at the other side of the room.

Marcus suddenly sat up straight and stared at my open exercise book.

'Can I copy your homework?' he said.

I was kind of cross because he'd scared Kellie away, and I felt like saying no. Then I looked a bit closer at Marcus. He wasn't wearing a jumper, and his school shirt was grubby and wrinkled. He looked kind of sick, and I couldn't help feeling sorry for him.

'Are you OK?' I asked.

'I feel a bit.....' he started to say, and then

he seemed to change his mind. 'Sure I'm OK,' he said in a tough voice. 'Not that it's any business of yours.'

I didn't know what to say to that, so I just slid my homework towards him, and watched as he copied down every single word.

* * *

At break-time I decided it was time I asked Louise some more about Marcus.

'What's there to tell?' she said. 'He's trouble. That's all you need to know.'

'I think he's kind of cute,' said Alice.

She was right. There *was* something kind of cute about Marcus – in a dangerous kind of way.

Louise sighed.

'OK, so he's cute. But he's still trouble.'

She stopped and thought for a minute.

'But I suppose it's not really his fault.'

'Why?' asked Grace.

'Well, his mum died a few years ago. I don't even remember her properly, and he probably doesn't either. He doesn't have any brothers and sisters. So it's just Marcus and his dad. I suppose it's kind of lonely for him.'

'That's awful,' said Alice.

She was right – it was awful. Poor Marcus – no wonder he didn't seem very interested in school. He was probably too busy being sad all the time.

I didn't have time to worry about him though. Just then the bell rang, and I had to run to get my books ready for the next three classes.

*　　　*　　　*

Before the first class started, Kellie walked quickly past my desk, without even looking at me.

A few minutes later, Marcus came and sat beside me. I remembered what Louise had said about him. I smiled at him, but he didn't smile back.

Mr Spillane must have had a bad weekend, because he was really cross. He kept giving out about stupid stuff. When one girl sneezed, he looked like he wanted to kill her. Then he walked past a desk and noticed that another girl didn't have a textbook and he nearly went ballistic. He stormed around the class checking to see who had books. Of course, Marcus, as usual didn't have one, and four others were missing books too. Mr Spillane started to shout.

'You're not babies anymore. Is it too much to ask that everyone have a book in class each day? You've had two weeks to get used to how the system works – and that should be quite long enough. I've made up my mind – anyone who doesn't have a textbook tomorrow will be taking home a note from me to their parents. Is that clear? If you can't cope with bringing books to class, maybe you'd be better off back in primary school.'

I put my head down. I *did* like secondary school – sort of, but part of me wished myself back to primary school where everything was so much easier.

At last lunch-time came. I pulled my lunch-box out of my school-bag, and stood up to go to the lunch room.

'What have you got for your lunch?' asked Marcus.

He had barely spoken to me at all that day, and I almost jumped when I heard his voice.

I hadn't checked, but I knew what was

likely to be in my lunch-box – all kinds of healthy stuff that Marcus would think was for losers.

'Er … you know … nothing special … just food,' I said.

'Can I have some?'

I gulped. After what Louise had said about him, I didn't like to say no. Maybe his dad hadn't bought any food for him. Maybe he was really hungry. Maybe that was why he looked so sick.

But could I possibly give him a houmous sandwich, or a bag of sprouted seeds?

Marcus was waiting for an answer, so I peeped inside the lunch-box. I could see a tub of chick peas, a bottle of carrot juice and two sandwiches.

I couldn't see what was in the sandwiches, but they didn't look too gross, and they didn't smell too bad.

'You can have my sandwiches, if you like,' I said, holding them towards him.

Marcus didn't need to be asked twice. He took the sandwiches from my hand.

'Ta,' he said, and then he went out of the room, eating the first of the sandwiches as he went.

After lunch he came up to me.

'Thanks, Megan,' he said. 'They were really nice sandwiches.'

I wondered was he joking.

Was this some kind of bullying that I wasn't clever enough to understand properly?

Marcus was smiling though, and I found that I believed him. He really did like the sandwiches. How weird was that?

I felt kind of bad that my mum had made those sandwiches especially for me, and I'd given them away. Then I figured that she'd be proud of me for helping someone else. She's always telling me to be generous to people who aren't as lucky as I am.

Then I felt a sudden lump in my throat at the thought of Marcus who had no mum to do anything for him – even to make him gross, healthy sandwiches.

Chapter eleven

Next morning we had Mr Spillane's class first. Even the thought of it made me nervous, as I stood at my locker and got my books ready for the first three classes.

What if I brought the wrong book to class by mistake?

Mum and Dad would kill me if I brought a note home from school. The only bad thing about having a phone was that they were forever threatening to take it from me as a punishment. If I brought a note home from a teacher, they'd probably take my phone and not give it back for about a hundred years.

I double-checked that I had the right books and went to class. Marcus was there before me. As usual he didn't have a book in front of him.

'Why didn't you bring your Geography book?' I asked as I sat down next to him. 'You're going to be in big trouble.'

Marcus shrugged.

'How could I bring a book, when I don't even have one?' he asked.

He spoke in a tough kind of voice, but something made me feel sorry for him again.

Why didn't he have a book?

Maybe his father wouldn't give him money for one?

Maybe his father gave him the money and he spent it on food?

'But Mr Spillane is going to write a note in your diary,' I said.

Marcus nodded.

'I know. And I'm going to be in so much trouble. It's going to be my fifth note. My dad will go crazy. He's really violent sometimes. He'll ...'

He didn't finish the sentence. I gulped. My dad wouldn't hurt a fly. I couldn't begin to imagine what a violent father would be like. Poor Marcus.

Just then Mr Spillane walked in to the room.

'I haven't forgotten my promise,' he said. 'I'm coming around to check who has managed the very difficult task of bringing their Geography book to class.'

He walked slowly around the room, checking every table. It was kind of creepy as everyone sat in total silence. Soon I could hear Mr Spillane's footsteps behind me. I made a sudden decision. I carefully slid my book over to Marcus's side of the desk. Marcus gave me a funny look, but he didn't say anything.

Mr Spillane was beside us.

'Megan?' he said in surprise.

I could feel my face going red.

'I'm very sorry, Sir,' I said. 'I was studying Geography at home last night, and I left my book in my bedroom.'

Mr Spillane folded his arms and looked at Marcus. 'Megan has forgotten her book, and you've managed to bring a book for once in your life? Is this a co-incidence, or is there something funny going on?'

Marcus didn't answer. I held my breath and hoped that Mr Spillane wouldn't open the book and see my name written inside.

I smiled and tried to look innocent.

'I'm really sorry,' I said. 'I'll bring my book tomorrow.'

Mr Spillane sighed.

'I'm surprised at you, Megan,' he said. 'But a promise is a promise. Take out your diary.'

He opened my diary and I watched as he wrote in his slanty handwriting. *Despite a strict warning, Megan has not brought her Geography book to class today. Please discuss this matter with her.*

I sighed. He didn't know what he was doing. Didn't he know how long my mum needs to discuss anything? She could lecture me for hours about this. And then she'd probably take my phone too.

Mr Spillane gave me back my diary.

'Get your parents to sign this,' he said. 'I'll be checking tomorrow.'

Then he went to the top of the classroom and started to write on the white-board.

Marcus smiled at me.

'Thanks,' he said. 'You're OK.'

And then I totally embarrassed myself by going as red as the cover of the book that had got me into so much trouble.

* * *

After class, Jane came over.

'That was your book that Marcus had, wasn't it?' she said.

I didn't answer.

'He's using you, you know,' she said, as she walked away with her new best friend.

Was she right?

Was Marcus just using me?

I wasn't sure. All I was sure of was that when he smiled and said I was OK, I didn't care if he was using me or not. I just wanted him to keep on smiling.

Chapter twelve

As soon as I got home, I took out my homework diary and showed the note to Mum. She read it a few times, like there was some hidden message in it that she couldn't make any sense of. Then she sat down at the kitchen table, like the shock was too much for her. In my pocket I gripped my phone, getting ready to hand it over.

'I can't believe my eyes,' said Mum.

'You're not in the school three weeks and already you're bringing notes home?'

I ran my fingers over the keys of my phone. I had waited so long for it, and I loved it so much. What would I do without it? How would I text my friends? Could life go back to the way it was before?

I decided I had to tell the truth. Well sort of the truth anyway – telling the real truth about Marcus would make things much, much too complicated.

'You see, Mum,' I began. 'I actually brought my book to class. I always do. I'm really careful about stuff like that. But the … er … person next to me didn't have a book. And that person has parents who are really, really strict and ……'

'And you lent her your book so she wouldn't get into trouble?' finished Mum.

I didn't correct her. She thought I'd lent

my book to a girl, and I wasn't letting her know she was wrong.

I nodded slowly. Mum didn't answer for a while. I wondered if that was a good sign. With my mum you can never be sure about that kind of thing.

After ages Mum gave a big sigh.

'I don't know what to say to you, Megan,' she said.

So don't say anything, and especially don't say that you're going to confiscate my phone.

After another long silence Mum spoke again.

'What you did was very kind, and I like to see that. On the other hand, I don't want the teachers getting a bad impression of you so early in the term. Anyway, maybe we can overlook things just this once, but if it happens again, your friend will just have to be brave and take her punishment. Or maybe you could help her to get organised, so it doesn't happen any more.'

I didn't answer. How could I help Marcus? His problems were so big I wouldn't even know where to start.

'Now get me a pen,' continued Mum. 'I'll sign your diary and I'll get Dad to sign it too as soon as he's home.'

I raced to get a pen before she had time to change her mind. Then I ran into my bedroom, took out my phone and looked at it.

It had been a narrow escape.

* * *

On the way to school in the morning, I started to tell Alice what had happened the day before. I'd just got to where Mr Spillane was promising to send notes home, when Alice grabbed my arm.

'Look,' she said, pointing. 'Look over there.'

I looked, but wasn't quite sure what I was supposed to be looking at.

'Over there,' said Alice. 'It's an old lady.'

She was right. There was an old lady standing on the edge of the footpath, but what was so interesting about that?

Alice went on to explain.

'Our religion teacher was telling us all about helping old people. She said sometimes they can't see or hear very well, so things that would be simple to us could be really hard for them.'

We were very near the old woman now.

'Look,' said Alice. 'The poor old lady can't get across the road. We have to help her.'

Before I could say anything, Alice was shouting in the old lady's ear.

'Don't worry,' she said. 'We'll help you.'

Then before the old lady could say anything, Alice took her arm and practically dragged her across the road. Because I couldn't think of anything else to do, I followed them.

As soon as we were all safely on the footpath, Alice let go of the woman's arm.

'No need to thank me,' she said. 'I'm happy to help.'

The woman waved her walking stick in Alice's face.

'What on earth are you going on about?' she said.

Alice looked at her, puzzled.

'I was helping you across the road,' she said.

The woman waved her stick even closer to Alice's face.

'You silly girl,' she said. 'I wasn't trying to cross the road. I was just waiting for the bus, and if I don't get back across soon, I'm going to miss it.'

Alice went red.

'I'm sorry,' she said. 'Will I help you back again?'

The woman shook her head crossly.

'No, thank you. I can manage perfectly well on my own.'

'But,' began Alice, 'our teacher said crossing roads can be hard for old people ...'

Now the woman laughed.

'Thank you, dear, but *I'm* not old. I'm only eighty-three!'

Then before Alice could say another word, the woman crossed the road just in time to catch the bus.

Alice turned to me.

'What are you laughing at?' she said.

I was laughing so much I couldn't answer. Alice looked mad for a second, but then she saw the funny side, and we both laughed until tears were pouring down our cheeks.

So I never told her the story about Marcus and the Geography book.

Maybe it was just as well.

Chapter thirteen

Two weeks later, there was an overnight trip to an adventure centre for all first-years. I was really excited – two whole days with no school!

When it was time to go, Mum came to our front gate to wave goodbye to Alice and me.

'Phone when you're leaving school,' she said. 'And phone when you get to the adventure centre, and phone before you go to bed, and phone ....'

I sighed. I was beginning to wonder if having my own phone was such a good idea after all.

Mum was still talking, '...... and phone if you don't feel well, and phone if you just feel like a chat, and ....'

'Muuuum,' I wailed, and Mum stopped talking.

'Too much?' she asked.

I nodded.

'Much too much. How about I just phone you when I get there?'

Mum nodded slowly.

'OK, but ....'

Alice saved me like she often has to.

'We'd better go or we'll miss the bus,'

she said.

So I gave Mum one more hug and raced down the road before she had time to say anything else.

* * *

Everyone was very excited as we gathered outside the school gates. Grace, Louise, Alice and I all got on to the first bus and sat together near the back. Just as we were settling down, I saw Marcus walking down the bus towards us. As usual, he was on his own. He seemed to be heading for the empty seat just in front of me. Suddenly I felt embarrassed. Usually I was happy enough to see him, but now I just wanted to hang out with my friends. Marcus stopped at the empty seat. Then he looked at Alice, Grace and Louise who were laughing at a stupid joke that Grace had just told.

Marcus shrugged.

'I think I'll sit down here,' he said, pointing towards the back of the bus.

I was glad to see him go, and that made me feel really, really bad.

As soon as we got to the adventure centre, we had to change into our oldest clothes and meet at the edge of the woods.

Our PE teacher, Miss Ryan, was waiting for us when we got there.

'You're going orienteering,' she said. 'Divide yourselves into teams of four.'

I quickly looked at Grace, Louise and Alice, but then the teacher continued.

'All teams are to be mixed – two boys and two girls.'

In the end, Alice and I went with two boys from her class, Josh and Luke. Grace and Louise teamed up with two boys I didn't know. The teacher explained the rules, and then she gave us all maps and control cards.

When it was our turn to go, Alice grabbed the map and raced off into the woods without even reading it.

Josh and Luke laughed.

'Is she always like that?' asked Luke.

I laughed too.

'Mostly,' I said. 'Now let's go, or we'll never see her again.'

The orienteering was *soooo* much fun. We got lost loads of times, but it wasn't scary like the time Alice and I had got lost in the forest in France. For one thing, we had a map, and even though none of us was very good at reading it at first, in the end we got the hang of it.

Luke and Josh were really funny, and I was kind of sorry they weren't in my class. Then I decided that it didn't matter. Without

Alice, I wouldn't have been brave enough to talk to them anyway.

It seemed like no time until we were at the finishing point. Somehow our group managed to come third, and won a box of chocolates between the four of us. Generous Alice insisted on sharing with everyone, so we only got one each. Mum would have been very happy about that.

We went back to the hostel and showered and changed, and when it started to get dark, the hostel workers lit a huge fire, and showed us how to cook potatoes and sausages in it. Alice said everything tasted like ashes, but I didn't care. I knew if I was at home I'd be eating organic lentil stew or something exciting like that.

When the potatoes and sausages were finished, we all just sat around the fire chatting and toasting marshmallows. After a while Marcus came along. In the flickering of the flames he looked a bit wild and a bit scary. He sat down beside Alice, Grace, Louise and me. Grace had been telling a joke but she stopped suddenly when Marcus showed up, and no one said anything for a while.

'Did you enjoy the orienteering?' I asked Marcus.

He shrugged.

'It was OK, I suppose,' he said.

There was another silence after that.

'Did you like the food?' I asked. I knew it was a stupid question, but I didn't care. The silence was starting to make me nervous.

Marcus shrugged again.

'It was OK, I suppose,' he said. 'But I'd have preferred one of your mum's sandwiches.'

Alice gave me a funny look, but didn't say anything.

Then there was a very long, embarrassing silence. I couldn't think of anything else to say, and it didn't look like anyone else could either.

In the end Marcus got up.

'Bye,' he muttered, as he walked back towards the hostel.

'He's weird,' said Grace as soon as he was gone.

'He's bad,' said Louise.

'What was he saying about your mum's sandwiches?' said Alice.

Now everyone stared at me. I hoped no one would notice my blush in the firelight.

'Come on,' said Alice laughing. 'Tell us everything.'

I knew Alice wouldn't give up until I answered.

'There's not much to tell,' I said. 'I gave him a sandwich once, and he seemed to like it. That's all. Are you saying there's something wrong with someone liking my mum's sandwiches?'

'No,' said Alice giggling.

I threw a marshmallow at her, pretending I was cross. She caught it and ate it, and then threw one back at me. Then we had a brilliant marshmallow fight, until the hostel workers said it was time to go to bed.

Chapter fourteen

All the girls were to sleep in a huge dormitory. Grace, Alice, Louise and I got four beds in the corner of the room. Before long the PE teacher came around to make sure we were all in bed, and to turn out the lights. As soon as she was gone, Alice sat up.

'Come on girls,' she whispered. 'Time for ghost stories.'

So the four of us sat on Grace's bed, and took turns to tell scary stories. Alice told a totally creepy story about a ghost and his pet boar, who ate a whole child every day. It was a stupid story, but Alice told it so well that I could feel goosebumps running up and down my arms.

Then Grace and Louise told stories; I knew it was my turn next. I couldn't make anything up, so I repeated a story I'd read the year before. No one guessed that I hadn't made it up, and I realised Mum was right whenever she tells me to – *read more, because you never know when stuff you read might be useful.*

After that we shared a huge bar of chocolate that Louise had brought, and when Alice couldn't stop yawning, we decided it was time to go back to bed.

I was just drifting off to sleep when I heard a funny snuffling noise. All I could think of was the boar in the story Alice had told. I know that boar don't really eat children, but it still made me shiver.

'Alice?' I called softly, but she didn't answer. She was breathing deeply and probably already asleep.

Now who would save me?

Then I listened a bit more and realised it wasn't an animal noise. It was a human noise and it was coming from the bed just next to mine.

I sat up and rubbed my eyes. In the dim light, I could see Jane curled up in bed, sobbing softly.

I climbed out of bed and tip-toed over to Jane.

'What's wrong?' I whispered. 'Are you

sick? Do you want me to call a teacher?'

Jane shook her head, still sobbing.

'Well, what is it?' I said a bit impatiently. I was tired, and the floor was cold under my bare feet.

Jane stopped sobbing for a second.

'I'm homesick,' she said. 'I've never been away from home before and I miss my mum and dad.'

At first I thought she was being a bit silly, but then I remembered the year before when I was staying in Dublin with Alice, and we had a fight, and I really, really wanted to go home.

So I tried to sound a bit kinder as I said, 'What about Lyndsay?' (Lyndsay was her new best friend.)

Jane pointed to the next bed along.

'She's there, but she's asleep.'

'Do you want me to wake her up? I bet

she wouldn't mind, and chatting to her might make you feel a bit better.'

And I'd feel a whole lot better if I could get back to my bed and get some sleep.

Jane shook her head quickly.

'No, don't wake her up. I don't want her to think I'm a baby.'

'So what do you want me to do?'

Jane wiped her eyes.

'Would you ... would you mind just staying here for a little while? I feel better now that you're here. Please?'

And what could I say to that?

So I sat on the edge of Jane's bed, curled my feet under me to try to keep them warm, and waited.

Gradually Jane's sobbing stopped. Every few minutes she opened her eyes, like she was checking to see if I was still there. It was kind of peaceful just sitting there in the half-dark, listening to the breathing of the other girls.

Jane was OK really. It was wrong of me to dismiss her just because she liked different stuff to me. In a way, I was sorry that she wasn't the kind of girl I wanted to be friends with. Then I decided she probably didn't want to be friends with me either, and I felt a bit better.

After a while, Jane's eyes hadn't opened for ages, and she was breathing deeply like someone who was sound asleep. I waited a few more minutes, just to be sure, then I tip-toed back to my own bed, and seconds later I was fast asleep and dreaming of burnt sausages, and yummy, warm marshmallows.

* * *

When I woke up in the morning, I looked

over towards Jane's bed. She was sitting up chatting happily to Lyndsay. Suddenly she turned around and saw me.

'Thanks, Megan,' she whispered.

I smiled at her.

'You're welcome,' I said, and then I couldn't say any more as Alice suddenly jumped on my bed and whacked me with her pillow, and we had a pillow fight until Miss Ryan came in to see what all the noise was about.

After breakfast (more sausages), we had time for one more activity before it was time to leave.

'Let's go canoeing,' said Alice.

I'd never been canoeing before, and it sounded a bit scary. As usual, Alice read my mind.

'Don't worry,' she said. 'I'll mind you.'

I know she was trying to make me feel

better, but it didn't really work.

We were kitted out in life-jackets, and the instructor helped us into a two-person canoe.

'Have you done this before?' he asked.

'Yeah, loads of times,' said Alice.

'OK,' said the instructor. 'Off you go then. Be back in an hour. I'll blow my whistle to let you know when it's time.'

Then he gave us a big push and we slid off towards the centre of the lake.

'When did you do this before?' I asked.

Alice laughed happily.

'Never.'

'So why ...?'

Alice laughed again.

'I just wanted to get started. I didn't want to listen to him going on and on. And anyway, how hard can it be?'

Actually it was very hard. We kept going

around in circles, and crashing in to the bushes at the edge of the lake.

'Are you OK girls?' called the instructor after a while.

We weren't, but of course Alice wasn't admitting that.

'Fine,' she called back. 'Just practising our strokes.'

The instructor laughed.

'Keep practising then,' he said, as turned to help another group.

'Where's your friend Marcus this morning?' said Alice after a while.

I'd seen him when we were walking towards the lake. He was sitting on the ground behind a tree, smoking. For some reason I didn't tell Alice this. I didn't want her to think badly of him.

So I just said, 'Don't know.'

Alice didn't ask any more – she was too

busy steering us into yet another bush.

Much later we heard the sound of the whistle calling us back. We had somehow managed to get to the other side of the lake, but we still hadn't figured out how to go in a straight line. There was no way we were going to get back to the jetty any time soon.

'Should we call the instructor?' I said. 'We shouldn't be late back.'

'No,' said Alice crossly. 'I'm just getting the hang of this.'

She paddled furiously, and we crashed into yet another bush, and I had to duck to avoid being whacked by a huge branch.

Just then Josh and another boy paddled by.

'Need help?' called Josh.

'No, thank you,' said Alice.

'Yes, please!' I said at the same time.

Luckily they listened to me.

'Throw us the rope that's tied to the front of your canoe,' said Josh.

Alice sulkily did as he suggested, and they pulled us clear of the bushes. Then they showed us how to paddle in time. Like most things, it wasn't so hard once you know how to do it properly, and by the time we got to the jetty, I was beginning to enjoy myself.

We just had time for a quick shower. Then we had lunch and it was time to leave. As Alice, Grace, Louise and I waited to climb onto one bus, I was kind of glad to see Marcus getting on to a different one.

We sang all the way home, and I felt totally happy until we pulled up outside the school, and I remembered that the next day I'd have to manage without my friends again.

Chapter fifteen

By the time Friday came around, I was really looking forward to Home Ec – my favourite part of the week. Alice was still a total disaster in the cookery room. Miss Leonard was starting to get used to her though, and once she realised that Alice wasn't deliberately making a mess of everything she touched, she was actually quite nice to her.

'I'll make a chef of you, Alice O'Rourke, if it's the last thing I do,' she often said. Secretly I hoped Alice's cookery skills wouldn't improve – Home Ec class wouldn't have been half as much fun then.

After school that Friday Grace, Louise, Alice and I walked home together. We were all going to the shopping centre. Grace and I were making Louise laugh by telling her about Alice's efforts to make custard.

'It was *totally* gross,' said Grace. 'There were lumps everywhere. It was like …'

'… yellow porridge,' I finished her sentence for her.

'It was Miss Leonard's fault,' protested Alice laughing. 'She should have allowed me to use the carton of ready-made custard, like Mum suggested.'

Now I laughed.

'I don't think opening a carton would count as a cookery lesson,' I said. 'That would be like getting a lesson in using a scissors, and I think we all learned that back in infants class.'

Louise sighed.

'I wish I'd done Home Ec with you. It sounds like sooo much fun.'

Just then Alice grabbed my arm and squeezed it tightly. Then she did the same to Louise. Lucky Grace had time to escape.

'Ow,' I said. 'That hurt, Alice. And I know you only did it so we'd stop going on about your lumpy custard.'

Alice shook her head.

'I didn't. Honest. Just look over there.'

We all looked where Alice was pointing, and then we all gasped.

'Is that ...?' asked Louise.

'Could it be ...?' began Grace.

'That's Melissa,' I said, without any doubt. I could tell by the way she was walking and by the way she was flicking her hair.

Before anyone could say anything else, Melissa was next to us.

'Hi, everyone,' she gushed. 'I'm home for the weekend. Isn't that totally great?'

Then before we could escape she hugged each one of us like we were her best friends in the whole wide world.

Then we all stood and looked at each other.

'So, Melissa, how's school?' asked Alice eventually.

Melissa looked at her like it was a trick question.

'Er, fine,' she said. Then she seemed to recover herself. 'I mean great. School is great. Totally great.'

'And how's the swimming pool, and the super-duper hockey pitch?' asked Alice.

'Great,' said Melissa. 'Everything's totally, totally great. You know, Madonna nearly sent her daughter to my school, but she changed her mind at the last minute. Did I tell you that before?'

'Only about a hundred times,' said Alice giggling.

Melissa didn't seem to notice that Alice was laughing at her.

'So where are you all going?' she asked.

'To the shopping centre,' said Louise.

Then there was another long silence. At last Alice smiled.

'Would you like to come with us?'

Melissa smiled back.

'I'd totally love that,' she said. So off we all went.

It was kind of weird. Grace and Louise

used to like Melissa, but now they don't.

Alice seems to like everyone in the world except for Melissa, and I'd always been a bit afraid of her.

And now we were all hanging out at the shopping centre like we were best friends.

After a while, Grace, Louise and Alice went to try on some clothes, and I found myself standing outside the dressing room with Melissa.

'So, is your new school really great?' I asked, trying to make conversation.

Melissa hesitated. 'Weeeell, yeeeees,' she said in the end.

'You don't sound very sure,' I said.

Melissa sighed.

'It's a really cool building, so that's great. And the swimming pool is great. And most of the girls are really nice, and that's great too. But ...'

'But what?' I asked, wishing the others would come out and rescue me.

Melissa lowered her voice.

'But …… sometimes I feel a bit lonely. I miss my friends from primary school. Sometimes I wish I was right back in Miss O'Herlihy's class. Do you think that sounds stupid?'

Of course I didn't think it was stupid. I knew exactly how she felt. Actually I often felt like that too.

I smiled at Melissa.

'I don't think that's stupid,' I said. 'I think it's brave of you to go to boarding school all on your own. Making new friends takes time, but you'll manage in the end. I bet everything will be great by the time Christmas comes.'

While I spoke I wondered if I was trying to convince Melissa or myself.

Melissa smiled at me.

'Thanks, Megan. Maybe you're right.'

All of a sudden, I wondered if I should confide in Melissa.

Should I tell her that, even though I was still best friends with Alice, I had no friends in my class?

Would Melissa understand the way I felt, in a way that Alice and the others didn't?

Or would she just laugh at me?

I decided to be brave.

'Er, Melissa,' I began. 'I know how you feel. Actually I feel—'

Just then my phone rang and I answered it. It was Mum.

'Tea's nearly ready, Megan,' she said. 'It's lovely chick-pea soup, so hurry home before Dad and Rosie eat it all up.'

'OK,' I said. 'I'll be home in ten minutes.'

I decided to try again. I turned back to Melissa.

'You know, I—', I began.

Once again I was interrupted, as the others came out from the changing rooms.

Suddenly Melissa didn't look sad any more. The old proud look was back on her face. I was glad I hadn't confided in her.

She flicked her hair over her shoulder, just missing my eye.

'What happened to your jacket, Megan?' she asked as I ducked.

I could feel my face going red. I had ripped my jacket the week before, but instead of buying me a new one, Mum had insisted on covering the rip with a big, flowery patch. I knew it looked stupid, but Mum insisted that I keep on wearing it.

'Er, it got ripped,' I said. 'My mum sewed it for me.'

Melissa rubbed the line of stitching. Her voice was all silky and sweet, like honey in my ear.

'Your mother is *soooo* good at sewing,' she said. 'You must be very proud of her.'

I could feel my face going even redder. I knew Melissa was mocking me. She was being totally horrible, and I couldn't think of a single clever thing to say.

Just then Alice came over. She folded her arms and turned to face Melissa with a bright smile.

'Pity your mother can't sew,' she said. 'Then she could do us all a real big favour and sew your mouth shut.'

Grace, Louise and I giggled. Trust Alice to find the perfect put-down. For once, Melissa was speechless. She opened her mouth but no sound came out.

Then she seemed to recover. She flicked her hair one more time, and showed us her perfect white teeth.

'This has been totally great,' she said. 'Shopping is my very favourite thing. But sorry guys, I won't be able to hang out with you tomorrow. I've got plans. Hope you're not too disappointed.'

Alice grinned.

'We're dreadfully disappointed, but we'll try to get over it.'

Melissa didn't seem to notice that Alice was mocking her. It was like she had a big hard shell around her that protected her from anything bad.

She gave us each a huge hug, and skipped off, flicking her hair as she went, and I went home to enjoy a giant bowl of chick-pea soup.

Lucky me.

Chapter sixteen

The next few weeks went very, very slowly. Even the days seemed long, dragging on and on forever. Sometimes I saw Alice, Grace and Louise at small break, but mostly there wasn't time. We always had lunch together, but during lunch, time seemed to speed up, and the forty-five minute break always seemed to be over just as it was starting. Then I had to leave my friends and go back to my own class.

Even though most teachers let us sit wherever we wanted, everyone stuck to where they had been sitting in the first few days. It was like there was some unwritten rule that we were all afraid to break. That meant that, whatever classroom we were in, Jane and Lyndsay sat together at the top of the class, Kellie and her friends sat by the window, and Marcus and I sat together in the middle of the room.

By now it was clear that Marcus and I had something in common – neither of us had any other friends in our class. If it weren't for each other, we'd have been total loners.

Most days Marcus missed at least one class. He always ended up in trouble over this, but he didn't seem to care. After a while I began to think he even liked being in trouble. It was like a weird way of looking for attention.

Sometimes I felt like Marcus and I were almost friends. Sometimes he came in to class and smiled at me, as if he really liked me. Sometimes though, he was cross and sulky, and I was kind of afraid of him. And how can someone be your friend if you're afraid of them?

Sometimes he was really funny. One day, during a really boring Geography class, Marcus slid his copy over to my side of the desk. He'd written something in huge letters on the open page – '*This class is torture. Dog-breath should be taken out and punished for cruelty to teenagers.*'

I grinned and carefully slid the copy back over to Marcus. Just then Mr Spillane looked down towards us.

'Is your copy actually open, Marcus?' he

said. 'Don't tell me you've actually done some work? Why don't you bring it up to me so I can take a look?'

I gulped.

What would Mr Spillane say if he saw what Marcus had written?

What would he say if he discovered that Marcus calls him *Dog-breath?*

Marcus might like being in trouble, but no one could like being in as much trouble as he was going to be in if Mr Spillane read what he had written in his copy.

I quickly put up my hand.

'Yes, Megan, what is it?' said Mr Spillane.

'Er ...', I said. 'Er ... do you know what that bird outside the window is called?'

Mr Spillane made an impatient sighing noise, and looked out the window.

'I don't see any bird. And besides, this is meant to be Geography, not bird-watching.'

There hadn't been any bird to see, but the distraction had been long enough for Marcus to carefully turn over the pages of his copy, hiding what he'd written. Now the copy was open on a page with a diagram on the formation of oxbow lakes.

He carried it up to Mr Spillane's desk. Mr Spillane studied the diagram carefully.

'Well, Marcus. I have to admit that I'm surprised. That diagram is actually very good. Maybe you're not a lost cause yet.'

He spoke very slowly, almost like it hurt him to say the words.

I put my head down and smiled.

Maybe Mr Spillane would have felt better if he knew that I'd drawn the diagram for Marcus the week before.

Marcus walked back to his desk, winking at me as he went.

At last the class was over, and it was

lunch-time. Marcus turned to me as I packed up my books.

'Thanks, Megan,' he said. 'It was really nice of you to save me from Dog-breath.'

I could feel my face going red.

'It's OK,' I said, reaching in to my bag for my lunch box. Then I stood up to go.

Marcus looked at my lunch-box.

'Any nice sandwiches today?'

I smiled.

'Probably not. But you can have them if you like.'

This was kind of like a private joke between us. Marcus ate my sandwiches most days. I didn't mind really. I was never very hungry at lunch time, and if I was, one of my friends would share with me.

I took out my sandwiches, and handed them to Marcus. As he reached out to take them, I noticed a huge black and yellow bruise on his wrist.

'What's that?' I asked, pointing.

'What's what?' he asked, pulling his jumper over the mark.

'That bruise,' I said. 'What happened to you?'

Marcus put his head down so that his long hair almost covered his face.

'It's nothing,' he said. 'Just a bruise. I can't even remember where I got it.'

I knew he was lying. No one could forget getting a bruise like that. It must have hurt like anything. But why would he lie? Why would anyone lie about a bruise?

'Thanks for the sandwiches,' he said quickly. 'See you later.'

As he walked out of the classroom, he turned and gave me a small smile. Suddenly I realised that even though Marcus often gave that small smile, he never really looked happy.

Had I ever heard him laugh?

I didn't think so.

As Marcus stopped at the classroom door to let some of the other boys out, I noticed once again how thin and tired he looked.

Who was this strange boy? I wondered.

And what could possibly be going on in his life?

Chapter seventeen

Then, at the beginning of December the real trouble started.

It was a Monday morning, a week before the Christmas exams. Instead of doing Geography, Mr Spillane decided to give us a big, long lecture.

'As you know,' he said. 'All four first year classes do the same exam, and I hope all of you in class M are going to make me proud by doing exceptionally well.'

Next to me Marcus started muttering.

'What is that man *on*? What kind of crazy

person would want to make Dog-breath proud? Maybe we should all deliberately fail, just to annoy him.'

I giggled, but stopped when I realised that Mr Spillane was looking straight at me.

Mr Spillane had lots more to say, all about the exams. I started to feel really bad. Once again I wished I was back in primary school. Back then exams seemed easy, and I always came near the top of my class. Secondary school was different though. There were so many subjects, and so much hard stuff to learn.

After class, Marcus didn't seem to think the exams were so funny any more. He didn't even get up to leave. He just sat there at his desk, blocking my way out of the classroom.

'I'm so, so dead,' he said. 'I haven't done any work for my exams. I'm going to fail everything. My dad's going to go crazy.'

'You've got a week left,' I said. 'If you work really hard, you could catch up.'

He shook his head.

'No, I couldn't.'

'I'll help you,' I said suddenly, without even thinking about it.

'How?' asked Marcus.

I had to think. Lunch-time was my favourite part of the school day, the only time I got to see my friends. But Marcus was in trouble, and who else was going to help him? So I spoke quickly, before I had time to change my mind.

'I'll go over stuff at lunch-time with you,' I said. 'We can do a different subject every day.'

Marcus looked happy for a second, then he shook his head slowly.

'Thanks, Megan,' he said. 'But that won't

work. I've left it too late. I'm doomed.'

Marcus gave a big moan and put his head in his hands. I could see the last straggly bits of purple that hadn't yet grown out of his hair. There was a small graze on the back of his neck. I lifted one hand, and for one weird second I felt like stroking his back to make him feel better. Then I got sense. This was Marcus Wall, the boy my friends thought I should be afraid of.

What would they say if they heard I was sitting in an almost-empty classroom, stroking his back?

So I put my hand in my pocket and took a deep breath to try to clear my head.

'What will happen if you do badly in your exams?' I asked after a while.

His voice was so muffled I could barely hear him.

'My dad will go totally ballistic,' he said.

Poor Marcus. He didn't talk about his dad very much – actually he didn't talk much about anything, but whenever he did say anything about his dad, he made him sound really scary. Would he really go crazy if Marcus did badly in his exams?

Anyone could see that Marcus had heaps of problems. He always looked sick and pale and tired. He never had any school-books, or proper uniform or lunch. He was always in trouble. If he failed his exams, would his problems just get worse?

Was there anything I could do to help him?

I felt like crying.

'Please let me help you,' I said. 'We could study after school. And maybe in the mornings too, before school starts. We could come in early. I could make notes for you to study at home. I could—'

Marcus sat up and rubbed his eyes. He looked old and worn-out.

'Thanks, Megan,' he said. 'That's really nice of you, but it wouldn't work. Like I said, I've left it too late. And besides, I'm not as clever as you.'

Was I clever?

I used to think I was, but secondary school was so confusing I couldn't even remember properly any more.

'So what are you going to do?' I asked.

Marcus smiled suddenly.

'Don't worry about me,' he said. 'I'll survive. I'm tough.'

Just then I realised something I'd never noticed before.

'You're not tough,' I said. 'You just pretend to be.'

Now it was his turn to go red.

I knew I was right.

Marcus didn't say anything for a minute. He just scratched the grazed patch of skin on his neck. I started to feel embarrassed.

'So what are you going to do?' I repeated.

Marcus stood up.

'I don't know yet, but I'll think of something. Remember, Megan, there's always a way.'

And with that strange comment he walked out of the classroom, closing the door quietly behind him.

Chapter eighteen

Marcus didn't show up for the next few classes, and I started to get a bit worried about him.

Was he going to do something stupid?

And if he did, what could I do about it?

I was really happy when he showed up before the last class of the day started.

'Hey, Megan,' he said. 'How's it going?'

He was grinning like he was having the best day of his life.

What was going on?

Had he forgotten about our conversation?

Had he forgotten all about the exams?

'You look very happy,' I said.

He nodded.

'Clever of you to notice. I *am* happy.'

'So you're not worried about the exams any more?' I asked.

He shook his head.

'Nope.'

'How come? You were really worried this morning. What's happened since then?'

He grinned again.

'I've figured out a way to get all 'A's.'

I sighed.

'Yeah, so have I. Work really hard.'

Marcus shook his head.

'That's one way. But that's the way for losers. Like I told you this morning, there's always another way. And I've found the easy way.'

Now I started to feel really worried.

There isn't an easy way to do well in exams.

So why did Marcus think there was?

And why was he looking so pleased with himself?

The teacher was late for class, and everyone was still standing around chatting. Marcus caught my arm and pulled me into a quiet corner.

'You know my friend, Gerry from fifth year?' he asked.

I shrugged. If you'd asked me, I'm not sure I'd have said that Marcus had friends. Usually when I saw him at break-time, he was on his own. Sometimes, he stood around with a group of older boys – scary-looking boys who were always in trouble. They never seemed to talk much, they just stood around looking tough.

'Anyway,' Marcus continued, not waiting

for my answer. 'Gerry was in the secretary's office today, waiting for Mrs Kingston to bring him to detention.'

I couldn't help smiling. Why wasn't I surprised that a friend of Marcus's was in detention?

Marcus didn't notice my smile as he continued to speak.

'When Mrs Kingston came in, she spent ages talking to the secretary about photocopying the exam papers, so they'll be ready for next week.'

Now I started to feel very worried. I could see Jane and her friend, Lyndsay, sitting at the top of the classroom testing each other on something from their maths books. Kellie and her friends were laughing at the back of the room.

So why was I stuck in a corner with a boy who was making me *very* nervous by talking about photocopying exam papers, and getting 'A's without actually doing any work?

Marcus didn't seem to notice that I wasn't saying anything, so he kept on talking.

'Gerry said that Mrs Kingston told the secretary that the teachers will have all the papers in the office by Wednesday. Then she asked the secretary to have them photocopied and ready for use by Thursday lunch-time.'

He gave me a big smile and folded his arms like he was finished his story.

Had I missed something?

'And?' I said.

Marcus gave a big sigh.

'The exams don't start until Tuesday of next week, and the exam papers are going to be in the secretary's office since this Thursday at lunch-time.'

I still didn't understand.

'And?' I said again, really wishing that this conversation was over.

Marcus gave an even bigger sigh.

'How easy do I have to make this for you? I get the exam papers. I read the exam papers. I learn the answers. I get all 'A's. Everyone's happy. End of story.'

I should have been cross that he was talking to me like I was a baby, but I had too many other things to think about.

'But …', I began. There were so many 'buts' running through my head, I didn't know which one to start with.

'But they'll notice if some papers are missing, won't they?' I said in the end.

Marcus shook his head.

'Mrs Kingston told the secretary to do a few spares, just in case. And no one's going to count them, unless they run out, and they won't run out, because I'll only get one of each paper!'

He was probably right.

'But, that's cheating,' I said after a while. 'That's not fair.'

Marcus shrugged.

'Lots of things aren't fair. Life's not fair. It's not fair that my mum died. It's not fair that my dad's a bully.'

He was right. Those things weren't fair, but did stealing the exam papers make everything right again?

I didn't think so.

I thought of another question.

'How are you going to get the papers?' I asked. 'You can't just walk in and take them. And I've watched the secretary – she never, ever leaves the office without locking the door behind her.'

Marcus shrugged.

'It's a secondary school office, not the

Bank of Ireland. There has to be a way to get those papers. And if there is a way, I'll figure it out.'

Now I was starting to feel really scared. I could feel a horrible cold chill on the back of my neck.

Why was Marcus telling me all of this?

Why wasn't he afraid that I'd tell someone?

Marcus looked at me closely, and I felt like he was looking right through my brain. He waggled his finger in my face.

'I know you wouldn't tell anyone about this, Megan. You wouldn't dare.'

Chapter nineteen

I was very relieved when Marcus didn't show up for school the next day. I had to sit on my own in class, but for once I didn't mind. Being on my own was easier than being with Marcus when he was talking of doing crazy stuff like stealing exam papers.

On the way home from school, Alice noticed that something was wrong.

'What's up, Megan?' she said. 'Even

you're not usually this quiet.'

I didn't answer. I so badly wanted to tell her what Marcus had said, but something made me afraid.

Alice would insist that I told someone, or she might even tell someone herself. And how could I let her do that?

If Marcus knew I'd told someone, he'd – well I don't know what he'd do, but I knew it wouldn't be nice.

And besides, as his dad was such a bully, maybe it was best if Marcus *did* steal the papers. It wasn't an honest thing to do, but at least it would stop his dad from going crazy. Marcus could do well in the Christmas exams, and in January, I could persuade him to do some school-work, and he'd continue to do well.

Maybe Marcus stealing the papers was a good thing?

But something told me that Alice wouldn't agree, so when she repeated, 'Come on, Meg, what's up?' I just shrugged.

'Nothing's up. I'm tired, that's all. Double Business Studies always has that effect on me.'

Alice laughed, and didn't notice that I was lying, and we talked about something else all the way home.

* * *

During dinner that night, all I could think of was Marcus.

Why couldn't he just study for his exams like a normal person would?

Why did he have to try to steal the exam papers?

And why did he have to tell me all about it?

* * *

After dinner, Mum gave me a bag of rubbish to carry outside. I opened the back door and shivered. It was damp and cold in the garden. The light from the kitchen window cast long shadows, making everything look really scary.

As I walked towards the bin, I glimpsed something small running into a corner at the side of the house. I jumped and screamed at the same time.

'Mum, Dad, help! Quickly, come and save me! *Heeeelp*!'

Mum raced out of the kitchen, drying her hands on her apron.

'What is it, Megan?' she said. 'Why are you screaming?'

Before answering, I dropped the bag of rubbish, and scrambled up onto the patio table.

Maybe I'd be safer up there.

Maybe whatever was running around the garden wasn't any good at climbing.

'It's … it's … I don't know what it is,' I squealed from my perch. 'But it's over there hiding behind that plant!'

Mum sighed.

'If it's small enough to hide behind that little plant, I suspect it's not terribly dangerous,' she said.

Then she went back towards the kitchen.

'Don't leave me here on my own,' I screeched. 'I thought you loved me.'

Mum turned back for a second.

'I *do* love you,' she said. 'That's why I'm not giving in to your drama queen antics.'

She went in to the kitchen, and seconds later she came out carrying the sweeping brush.

'It's probably just a mouse,' she said. 'You lift up the plant, and I'll chase it away with the brush.'

I shook my head.

'No *way*!' I said.

'Don't be such a coward, Megan,' said Mum.

'I'm not doing it,' I said. 'It's probably a rat, and if it jumps up and bites me and I die from a horrible disease, you'll be really sorry.'

Mum gave me a cross look.

'Go over and lift up that plant now, or else I'll know you're not mature enough to have a phone, and I'll have to take it from you.'

I knew I was beaten.

What did I ever do to deserve such an evil mum?

I took a deep breath and climbed down from the table. I tiptoed over to the plant, leaned over, and very slowly pushed it aside with my foot. I was ready to race away and climb back on to the patio table, if the creature tried to attack me.

Then nothing happened.

I took another deep breath and leaned a bit closer. It was hard to see properly, because there was a big shadow blocking my view. As I got used to the dark, I could see two small eyes staring up at me.

'What is it?' asked Mum.

'I don't know,' I whispered. 'But it's got two eyes.'

'All the better to see you with,' said Mum. 'Now step back and I'll try to chase it out with the brush.'

I stepped back. Mum raised the brush, and just as she was about to strike, the creature crept out into the light.

I gasped.

It wasn't a rat.

It wasn't a mouse.

It was a tiny, tiny kitten – a tiny, black kitten, with one small flash of white on the tip of its tail. It was looking at me with huge, unblinking green-blue eyes. I decided it was probably the sweetest thing I had ever seen in my whole life.

Mum put the sweeping brush down, and the small clatter it caused made the kitten jump, and step backwards again.

I tiptoed closer. The kitten was so scared that it looked like it was trying to make itself disappear into the ground. I bent down and put out my hand.

'It's OK, kitty,' I said. 'I won't hurt you.'

Mum came over and stood beside me.

'It's a kitten,' she said.

Duh. Like I hadn't noticed.

I didn't say this though, because I was too excited.

'Do you think I should pick it up?' I asked.

Mum laughed.

'I think you could probably chance it,' she said. 'The poor little scrap doesn't exactly look like a killing machine.'

I edged closer, reached out and carefully picked up the creature. It was the softest thing I had ever touched. I rested it on one arm, and used the other hand to stroke it. At first it was trembling so much I felt like crying. After a few seconds though, it stopped shaking and began to purr. It looked up at me with its huge eyes, and I knew that I had just fallen in love.

I turned to Mum.

'Please, please, please, *please* can I keep it?' I asked.

Mum hesitated.

'You know I don't like cats very much,' she said.

'But I'll feed it and mind it. I'll do

everything,' I said. 'You'll never have to do a single thing for it.'

'It won't always be a kitten, you know,' said Mum. 'Very soon it will be a cat, and it won't be as cute as it is now. Will you still love it then?'

I nodded.

'I will. I'll always love it. Please Mum—'

'It couldn't live in the house,' said Mum, interrupting me.

I shook my head.

'It wouldn't have to,' I said. 'It can sleep in the garage. And I'll make a bed for it out of some old clothes, and …… please, please, *please*, Mum. Please let me keep it.'

Mum thought for a minute.

'It might belong to someone. We'll have to ask around.'

'I'll ask tomorrow, I promise. I'll knock on every single door on the road. And if it belongs to someone, I'll give it straight back. But it's probably a stray. And please, *please* Mum. Can I keep it?'

Mum smiled.

'I suppose you've persuaded me,' she said. 'Look. It's fallen asleep in your arms,' she said. 'I think it's decided that you're its mother.'

'Thanks, Mum,' I said, as I cuddled my sleeping baby. 'This is the best thing that has ever happened to me.'

Half an hour later, I had made a bed for the kitten in an old shoe-box in the garage. Dad had looked closely at it and decided that she was a girl. I fed her warm milk and mashed up bread, and stroked her and cuddled her. I decided to call her Domino. And I decided that Domino would be the most-loved kitten in the history of the world.

And when I went to bed that night, I

realised that I hadn't thought about Marcus, or the exams, for hours and hours.

Chapter twenty

In the morning, I got up early so I could feed Domino and play with her before school. I sat in the cold garage and hugged her.

'I have to go to school soon,' I said. 'And I'm not looking forward to it. You see there's this boy, Marcus. Sometimes he's nice, and sometimes he's scary.'

I kept talking until I'd told Domino the

whole story. It felt a bit stupid, talking to a kitten, and of course I knew she couldn't understand me. She just stared up at me with her shining eyes, but in a way it helped me to sort things out in my mind. After ten minutes with Domino, I knew exactly what I had to do. It was very simple really – all I had to do was persuade Marcus not to steal the exam papers.

* * *

Alice called for me to walk to school, so I brought her out to the garage to show her my new pet.

'She's sweet,' she said, but I knew she was just saying that to please me. She doesn't like cats very much. I didn't mind. In a way I was kind of glad that Alice didn't like her. Now Domino would be my special, special pet, and I wouldn't have to share her with anyone.

*   *   *

When I got to my classroom, Kellie was sitting on her own – her friends weren't there yet. She smiled over at me. Most days we said 'hi' to each other, but we never managed to get past that. I wondered if I should go over and tell her about Domino. Lots of Kellie's books had pictures of cats on them, so maybe she was really interested in cats. Maybe this was the way for me to get to know her?

And now that she was on her own, it was the perfect opportunity.

I had taken just one step towards her when Marcus came in to the room. As soon as Kellie saw him, she stopped smiling, and started to take out her books. I sighed. Why couldn't I ever get the chance to talk to her?

I went to my desk and sat down, and as usual, Marcus sat beside me. He was even paler than usual, and kind of jumpy-looking.

This was my chance to tell him not to steal the papers. I didn't know how to start though. I couldn't organise the right sentences in my head. All the words seemed jumbled up, and I knew I wouldn't be able to say them properly.

Then, before I could say a single word, Marcus spoke.

'It's all sorted,' he said.

'What's all sorted?' I whispered, like I didn't know.

'Getting the exam papers. I have a perfect plan. I—'

Just then the teacher walked in to the class. She rapped her knuckles on her desk, and Marcus stopped talking. I looked at my book and tried to concentrate, but couldn't.

I was well used to crazy plans – after all, Alice had spent most of the previous year thinking up mad ideas to try to get her parents together. But this was different. This was very, very different. Alice had done a few stupid things, but she'd never, ever done something as bad as what Marcus was suggesting.

The class seemed to go on forever, and I couldn't listen to a single word the teacher was saying. Halfway through the class, I noticed that the room had become completely silent. I looked up and realised that everyone was staring at me. No one was talking, and the only sound was from the teacher's pen rapping impatiently on her desk. The teacher must have asked me a question, but I had no idea what it was. I could feel my face going bright red. I looked desperately at Marcus, but he was no help to me. His head was down, and he was busy drawing a huge spider on the back of one of his exercise books.

'Er,' I muttered. 'I …'

Suddenly there was a funny hissing sound from the front of the classroom. I looked up and saw that Jane had turned around in her desk, and was trying to get my attention.

'The Ancient Romans,' she whispered.

'Er, the Ancient Romans,' I repeated.

'That is correct, Megan,' said the teacher. 'Just be a bit quicker next time please.'

Then she moved on to someone else.

Jane was still looking at me.

'Thanks,' I whispered.

She shrugged, and turned back to her book.

I knew it was going to be a very long morning.

Chapter twenty-one

Somehow I got through the next two classes. Between the classes, Marcus vanished as usual, so I had no chance to talk to him. As soon as the last teacher left the room, I stood up to go outside.

Marcus stood up too.

'Wait Megan,' he said. 'Don't you want to hear my plan?'

I think the last thing in the whole world I wanted to hear right then was Marcus's plan.

How could I tell him that though?

And how could I leave when Marcus was blocking my way out of the classroom?

Except for Marcus and me, the classroom was empty, as everyone rushed off to enjoy their break.

'Er ... Marcus, ... I think I need to go now,' I said. 'I've got to ...... I've got to go.'

Still Marcus didn't move. He had a funny look in his eyes, and I was starting to feel scared.

'Let me tell you my plan,' he repeated.

I shook my head. Suddenly I knew what I had to say, and the words came tumbling out.

'No, Marcus,' I said. 'I'm not interested in your plan. Whatever it is, it's a stupid plan. You shouldn't steal the papers. It's wrong, and in the long term, it won't change anything. You should just do your best, and if you fail – get over it, and do better the next time.'

'Let me tell you my plan,' he said again.

Once again I shook my head.

'Can't you understand? I don't want to know *anything* about your stupid plan. If you tell me, that makes me guilty too, and I'm not letting that happen. I'm not getting involved, just because you're too lazy to do any work. So forget it, OK? It's not going to happen.'

I stopped for breath. I think we were both surprised at my outburst. Suddenly I was afraid.

What was Marcus going to do now?

We looked at each other for a minute, then Marcus slowly shook his head.

'You just don't understand,' he said quietly, and then he picked up his bag and walked out of the classroom.

*　　*　　*

Marcus didn't show up for the rest of the day, and I was really glad about that.

When I got home, I raced out to the garage to play with Domino. I'd left the door a little bit open so she could go outside to play, but she was curled up inside in her shoe-box, where it was nice and warm. I picked her up and snuggled her against my chin. Just holding her made me feel better. She licked my finger with her rough, sandpapery tongue, and made soft mewing noises. I could feel her heart beating gently against my hand.

Then Mum came out.

'Don't forget you have to ask around, to see if that kitten belongs to someone,' she said.

'But *Mum*!' I wailed.

What would I do if I had to give Domino away?

Already she felt like she was mine, losing her would be too cruel to even think about.

Mum was firm.

'I insist,' she said. 'I know you love her, but you have to think how you would feel if someone else took her. Just call to every house on the road, and ask, and if no one owns her you can keep her. That's the deal.'

I knew there was no point in arguing, so I called for Alice, and she agreed to help me.

The first three houses were easy – no one had lost a kitten. The next house was Mrs O'Callaghan's. Alice made a face when Mrs O'Callaghan came to open the door. I knew Alice was remembering when she was hiding in my house last year, and she overheard Mrs O'Callaghan saying mean stuff about her mum.

'What do you two want?' said Mrs O'Callaghan crossly.

'We were wondering if you've lost a kitten,' I said quietly.

'Actually, I have,' said Mrs O'Callaghan.

I gulped.

Would I have to lose my precious Domino?

Would I have to give my darling kitten to this nasty, mean old woman?

Just then there was a hoarse mewing sound, and a huge, battered-looking ginger cat came out from a bush beside us. It went up to Mrs O'Callaghan and rubbed against her bony legs.

'There you are my little baby,' said Mrs O'Callaghan. 'I haven't seen you all day. Were you a naughty little kitty, running away from your mummy like that?'

Alice made a big show of pretending to get sick in the bush, but Mrs O'Callaghan was too busy rubbing her cat's straggly fur to notice.

'Run along, girls,' she said. 'My baby is back now.'

I was very happy to run along, and as soon as we were safely on the street, Alice and I laughed until we cried.

The people in the next few houses knew nothing about a lost kitten, and I was starting to feel better as we walked up the path to the last house on our road.

'Who lives here?' asked Alice.

'A man and his wife,' I said. 'They only moved here last week. I've never met them before. They're Polish.'

'Leave this to me, then,' said Alice. 'I'm good at sign language.'

'Maybe they speak English,' I said, but

before Alice could answer, the door was open and the man was standing looking at us.

'Did ...... you ...... lose ...... a ...... cat?' asked Alice in a very slow and very loud voice.

Then before the man could reply, Alice put on a sad face, and started miaowing softly.

The man folded his arms, and stared at Alice like she was crazy. She didn't seem to notice.

'CAT ... LOST,' she shouted so loudly that the man had to take a step backwards.

Then he shouted back at her.

'Cat!' he said. 'I ... like ... cat. Is ... my ... favourite ... food. Yum ... Yum!'

I gasped.

How could I keep Domino away from this mad, cat-eating man?

Suddenly the man started to laugh.

'I am making a joke,' he said. 'I am not deaf. I can speak English. I do not eat cats. I have not lost a cat. Do you want anything else?'

I giggled.

'No, thanks,' I said.

Then I grabbed a very red-faced Alice and we ran all the way back out on to the street.

'How was I supposed to know?' asked Alice, but I was too busy laughing to answer her.

That night I sneaked Domino in to my bedroom, and she slept curled up on the end of my bed. When she was next to me, the whole Marcus thing didn't seem so bad.

Chapter twenty-two

First thing in the morning, I sneaked Domino out through my bedroom window. She didn't want to go. I knew how she felt – I would have liked to stay curled up in my bed too.

Marcus didn't talk to me at all during the first three classes. He just sat there looking pale and scary.

When break-time came, everyone else got up and left the classroom. I couldn't take it any more.

'I'm sorry, Marcus,' I said. 'I'm sorry that you haven't studied for your exams. I'm sorry you're all mixed up. I'm—'

He put up his hand to stop me.

'Forget it,' he said. 'I don't want to know.'

'Fine,' I said impatiently. 'I've forgotten it already. Now excuse me, please, I want to go and meet my friends.'

I pushed past him, and as I did so, one of my arms brushed against his side.

Suddenly Marcus moaned. Then he doubled over, kind of crumpling down on to the chair he'd just been sitting on.

I felt a sudden flare of anger.

What was he on?

I'd barely touched him.

Surely he didn't expect me to believe that I'd hurt him?

He always acts so tough, so how could

brushing past him actually hurt?

But why wasn't he saying anything?

And why was his face even paler than ever – almost as white as the white-board at the top of the classroom?

'I'm so sorry, Marcus,' I said. 'I didn't mean. I—'

Marcus shook his head.

'It's not you. You didn't do anything.'

'Then why …?' I didn't know how to finish.

Marcus stood up, holding his side. He gave a funny smile that made him look even sadder than before.

'Don't worry,' he said. 'It'll be better before too long.'

'What will be better?'

'This,' he said, and as he spoke he lifted up the side of his shirt.

Now it was my turn to sit down quickly.

There was a gross black and blue bruise all down one side of Marcus's body. Even looking at it gave me a funny pain in my own side. My head went all woozy, and I felt like I was going to faint.

'What … what happened?' I asked as soon as I felt brave enough to talk.

'My dad,' Marcus said quietly. 'He … he …'

'He what?'

'Well it was my own fault really,' said Marcus. 'I should have known not to go bothering him when he was tired. He's always worse then. He's …'

He stopped talking, and tucked his shirt back into his trousers. I was glad not to be looking at the gross bruises any more, but I couldn't forget them just because they were now hidden by Marcus's not-very-clean school shirt.

'You have to tell someone,' I said. 'You have to tell the police. Or a doctor. Or a teacher, or someone. There has to be *someone* you can tell.'

Marcus shrugged.

'Why would I want to tell?'

'So they could help you, of course.'

Marcus shook his head.

'If they knew about this, they wouldn't let me live with Dad any more.'

'Wouldn't that be a good thing? If he … I mean … if he …', I stopped and pointed at Marcus's side.

'Dad's all I've got. I haven't got any other family. If I don't live with Dad, I'd have to go to a foster home or something, and I so wouldn't want to do that.'

'So what are you going to do?'

He shrugged again.

'Nothing. If I don't annoy him, this kind

of thing won't happen again. If I do really well in my Christmas tests, Dad will be pleased, and he'll leave me alone all through the holidays.'

I gulped.

'So you're really going to go through with it? You're really going to steal the exam papers?'

He nodded.

'I have to. I don't have any other choice.' Before I could think of an answer, he continued, 'And you're going to help me.'

And as I looked at him standing there, pale and tired and sick-looking, there was only one possible thing I could say.

'OK,' I whispered, and it was settled.

Chapter twenty-three

This was the scariest thing that had ever happened to me.

This was scarier than when Alice and Hazel sneaked out from summer camp.

It was even scarier than when Alice and I got lost in the forest in France.

Why had I agreed to help Marcus?

But what would happen to him if I didn't help him?

And what would happen to me if I did?

* * *

At lunch-time, I found myself sitting in the secretary's office. The plan was that I was supposed to pretend to be sick. I didn't have to pretend though – I really felt like I was going to throw up any second.

'You poor little scrap,' the secretary said. 'It's so awful when you don't feel well, isn't it.'

I nodded, too nervous to be cross with her for speaking to me like I was five.

'Now here's the phone,' she continued. 'Just give your mum a quick call, and she can come and pick you up and take you home to your own lovely, warm bed.'

Marcus had thought of everything, and he had told me exactly what to do next. I took the phone from the secretary, and I dialled my own mobile number. I knew that my mobile phone was switched off in my pocket, but even so, I was half afraid it was going to ring.

I handed the phone back to the secretary.

'It's busy,' I said.

She smiled at me.

'Oh dear. Is your mum a bit of a chatter-box? You can try again in a few minutes. You just sit there and relax.'

Sit there and relax?

I was in the middle of the worst thing I'd ever done in my whole life, and she expected me to relax?

The secretary returned to her work, and I sat there, trying not to throw up all over her office.

Behind the secretary, I could see a set of shelves lined with stacks of pages.

Suddenly I understood the true horror of

what I had agreed to do. My hands started to shake so much I had to sit on them to try to make them stop.

My parents would never, ever forgive me if they ever heard about this.

And I wouldn't blame them.

Even Alice, who often did bad stuff, would never forgive me for this.

I was just about to do a very, very bad thing.

Maybe I should stand up, tell the secretary I felt better and walk out of the room?

Suddenly I remembered Marcus's pale face, and the dark, black bruise on his side.

What would I tell him if I changed my mind?

And what would he tell his father when he failed his Christmas exams?

And what would his father do to him?

I tried to breathe deeply to calm myself

down, but it didn't work. I could hear funny gasping noises, and it took me a few seconds to realise that they were coming from my own mouth.

The secretary looked up.

'You poor little—', she began, but she didn't finish her sentence.

Just then there was loads of shouting in the corridor outside the door.

'What on earth is that noise?' said the secretary. 'It sounds like the school is falling down.'

I knew what the noise was, but I wasn't about to tell the secretary. I knew that it was Marcus and one of his friends, deliberately making noise, creating a distraction.

The noise got louder, and there was a huge crash, as if someone had been pushed into a wall.

The secretary jumped to her feet, opened

the door and looked out.

'Oh my goodness, it's a fight,' she said. 'Stop it right now, you bold boys!'

Then she stepped outside into the corridor and I watched in horror as the door closed softly behind her.

This was my chance.

Whether I liked it or not.

I stood up, wondering if my legs would be strong enough to hold me up. I tip-toed past the secretary's desk, to the shelves. There, just as Marcus had predicted, were neat piles of exam papers. The row nearest to me was labelled 'First Year'. Then each stack was labelled by subject. I glanced over my shoulder. The door was still closed, but from outside I could hear grunts and moans and funny bumping noises.

It was now or never.

Never felt like the best option. I ran back

to where I had been sitting, sat down and closed my eyes. I wasn't brave enough. I would never be brave enough to do something like this.

Suddenly the picture of Marcus's bruised side flashed into my mind again. Right now, he was outside the secretary's door, probably picking up more bruises, just so he wouldn't get into more trouble with his dad. He was depending on me, and it wasn't fair to let him down.

I took a deep breath, trying unsuccessfully to steady myself. Then I stood up again, and walked over to the piles of exam papers. Taking another deep breath, I reached out and grabbed one sheet from the top of each pile in the first year row. Then I raced back to my seat and stuffed the pages into my schoolbag.

Just as I was fastening the clasps on my

bag, the door opened and the secretary came in. She was all hot and nervous-looking.

'Well, I'm glad that's all over,' she said. 'It's lucky the principal came along when she did. What on earth were those silly boys thinking of, starting a fight right outside my office door?'

I don't think she expected me to answer this, so I didn't.

Then she continued.

'And you, you poor little girl. I hope those bold boys didn't frighten you?'

I was very frightened, but not because of the fight, so again I didn't reply.

She reached for the phone.

'Here, dear,' she said. 'You can try to ring your mother again.'

I shook my head.

'Actually I feel a bit better now,' I said.

'Maybe I just needed a little rest. I think I might go back to class now.'

She looked surprised.

'Are you sure?' she said.

I nodded, trying to look healthy.

'Sure, I'm sure. Whatever it was is better now. I'm fine, really.'

She smiled at me.

'If you're sure. But remember, if you feel sick again, just drop in and let me know.'

Then, feeling really, really bad, I stood up and opened the door.

There was no one outside in the corridor.

'Er, where are the boys who were fighting?' I asked the secretary.

'Oh, you poor little thing,' she said. 'Are you afraid to go out there? Are you afraid you're going to meet those boys?'

No. Actually I want to meet them, so I can give one of them this bundle of exam papers that I've just stolen from your office.

Before I could think of a good reply, she spoke again.

'You don't have to worry about them. They're gone to Mrs Kingston's office, and I expect they're going to be there for a very long time.'

So now I had to wander around the school for the afternoon with a set of stolen exam papers in my bag.

Great.

*   *   *

Marcus didn't show up for any classes after lunch. After school was over, I hung around Mrs Kingston's office for a while, hoping that he would appear. He didn't though, and I was too afraid to ask anyone if they'd seen him.

I knew Mum would soon be sending out

a search party for me, so I set off for home. My school-bag felt heavier than it ever had before. It pulled down on my shoulders like there was an elephant inside. I half-felt that the papers were going to burn a hole right through the bag, and that soon I would be walking along in a huge cloud of smoke.

Mum was in the kitchen when I got home.

'Hi, love,' she said. 'Did you have a nice day?'

I felt like running over to her and telling her everything, but how could I do that?

So I just muttered, 'Fine, thanks,' and went to my room before she could protest.

Once I was safely in my bedroom, I opened my bag, took out the exam papers and put them on my desk.

A new thought came to me.

Should I look at the papers?

After all, I'd taken the risk and stolen them, so why shouldn't I read them, and get fantastic marks in my exams?

And then, all of a sudden, I realised once again what a very, very bad thing I had done.

I grabbed the papers, and shoved them under my mattress.

Then I ran out of the room, slamming the door behind me.

I went out to the garage, picked up Domino and hugged her. She was as soft and warm and cuddly as ever, but it was no good. Even hugging Domino couldn't make me forget what I had done.

Chapter twenty-four

I had terrible nightmares that night. All night long I dreamed I was being chased by teachers waving bundles of exam papers at me, and screaming that I was a cheat.

In my dreams that night, even Domino didn't love me any more.

In the morning Mum came and shook my arm to wake me up.

'I didn't do it. I didn't do it,' I shouted.

Mum laughed.

'Didn't do what? Did you do something bad in your dreams? Do we need to take your phone from you to punish you?'

I opened my eyes and closed them again quickly when I saw Mum smiling down at me. If my parents ever discovered what I had done, they wouldn't just take my phone. They'd take my phone, and anything else they thought might make me happy, and they'd make a huge bonfire of them. Then they'd ground me for a few thousand years.

Mum laughed again.

'Come on, sleepyhead. Forget your dreams. It's time to get up for school.'

I shook my head.

'I can't get up, Mum. I'm sick.'

Mum leaned over me and looked closely at me.

'You know, Megan, you do look sick,' she said. 'Maybe you should stay at home today.'

Mum never, ever falls for it when I pretend to be sick. Only thing is, I wasn't pretending. I really did feel sick. I felt sicker than I ever had before. Even the thought of going to school made me feel all weak and shaky.

Mum rubbed my forehead.

'You go back to sleep for a while, and later on I'll bring you a nice warm drink.'

Then she suddenly looked worried.

'Oh, but what about your exams?' she said. 'You know they're on next week, don't you?'

Of course I knew the exams were next week. After all, the papers were stacked up under my mattress.

I sighed.

'I'll just have to work extra-hard at the weekend,' I said.

Mum smiled.

'I know you will. You're a good girl,

Megan. Dad and I are so proud of you.'

Then she went out of the room, and I turned my face into my pillow and cried myself back to sleep.

* * *

I woke up to a beeping sound – my mobile phone. I looked at the time. It was half-past ten, break-time at school. There was a text from Alice.

Called 4 U. Ur mum said U R sick. Hope not 2 bad.

I texted back.

Thanks.

I couldn't manage to say any more.

Just as I sent the message, my phone beeped again. This time the message was from Marcus. The sight of his name flashing up on my phone gave me a pain in my stomach. I opened the message. It was very short.

Where R U?

I felt like throwing my precious phone out the window. I didn't though. I knew I had to reply.

Am at home. Very sick.

I typed with shaking hands.

Seconds after I had sent the message, Marcus's reply came.

B at skool on Monday. Or else...

Or else what?

I didn't like to think what he meant, but I knew it wasn't anything nice.

Even though I was in my own bed, in my own house, I felt like I wasn't safe any more.

Just then Rosie came in. She jumped on to my bed, and then crawled in under the covers.

'Will I cuddle you until you're all better?' she asked.

I felt like crying.

Why couldn't life be simple any more?

All the cuddles in the world couldn't make me better.

Then Mum came in.

'Megan, if you're sick, maybe you should turn your phone off,' she said.

For once she was right. If I left my phone on, I might get another text from Marcus, and I *so* didn't want that. So I switched off my phone and put it on the floor next to my bed.

Mum sat down beside me and felt my forehead.

'Feeling any better?' she asked.

If anything, I felt worse, but I didn't say that to Mum.

I nodded.

'I think I'm a little bit better,' I said.

'Well enough for a nice big bowl of porridge?' she said.

I shook my head.

'No. Not that much better,' I said. 'But I might manage one small slice of toast.'

Mum patted my arm.

'I think we can arrange that,' she said.

She didn't get up to go.

'Rosie, why don't you go and pick out a jigsaw for you and I to do in a minute?' she said.

Rosie crawled out from under the covers, and I could hear the clump of her feet as she went upstairs.

'So, Megan, how are things at school these days?' Mum asked.

While she spoke, she was rubbing my back like she used to when I was really small. Her hand was warm, and kind of comforting.

Suddenly I really, really wanted to tell her about Marcus, and his dad, and the bruises, and …… everything. I even wanted to tell her about the exam papers and how I had stolen them.

But how could I do that?

How could I confess to doing such a very bad thing?

Mum might try to understand, but she'd still punish me.

She couldn't just ignore the fact that I'd done the very, very, very worst thing in my whole life.

She couldn't ignore the fact that I was a huge, huge disappointment to her.

'Well?' asked Mum.

I tried to smile.

'It's OK,' I said.

'And do you still sit next to that boy, Marcus, I think you said he was called?'

'Oh him?' I said, like Marcus hadn't been the centre of my thoughts for the past couple of days. 'Sometimes I sit next to him. But sometimes I sit next to other people.'

It wasn't really a lie. I sat next to Grace and Alice for Home Ec class.

'So you're a bit happier at school these days?' she asked.

Once again I was tempted to tell her the truth.

Once again I lied to her.

'Sure, Mum,' I said. 'Everything's fine. Couldn't be better.'

Mum patted my arm.

'I'm really glad,' she said, and then she went out to make my toast, before I could find the words to tell her the truth – that things couldn't possibly be any worse.

Chapter twenty-five

Next morning I woke up after another long, horrible night of nightmares. I leaned out of bed, picked up my phone and turned it on. There were six unread messages in my inbox. Three were from Alice, Grace and Louise, all hoping that I was feeling better. I felt a sudden sick feeling in my stomach when I saw that the last three were from Marcus.

I opened the first one. It was short.

Don't forget.

(Like I was ever, ever going to forget.)

The second message was longer.

If you don't bring what I want to skool on Monday I am in a lot of trouble ...

With shaking hands I opened the last message:

... but not as much trouble as you.

I switched off my phone again.

What was I going to do?

* * *

Shortly afterwards, I heard the doorbell ring. I heard Mum opening the door and then I could hear Alice's voice in the hallway. I was kind of tempted to call out to Mum that I was too sick for visitors, but before I could say anything, Alice was in my room.

'Hey, Meg' she said. 'Are you better yet? I wanted to call over last night, but Mum wouldn't let me. Grace and I really missed you in Home Ec yesterday. I'm getting better though. I managed to crack three whole eggs, without any getting on the floor. Miss Leonard said there might be hope for me after all.'

I had to smile. Alice wasn't pretending. She really was proud about the eggs, even though she'd just managed to do what Rosie had been able to do since she was three.

She came over and stood by my bed.

'So, Meg, are you really sick, or are you just faking?'

'I'm really si—' I started to say, but I couldn't finish. Instead of words, sobs were coming out of my mouth, and tears started to pour down my face.

Alice looked at me in alarm.

'Hey,' she said. 'I was just kidding. You know that, don't you?'

Of course I knew she was kidding, but I couldn't answer, I was still sobbing too much.

Now Alice sat on the edge of my bed. She looked really scared and I couldn't blame her – I must have looked totally scary.

'What's happened?' she said. 'Please tell me what's wrong? Do you want me to go and get your mum?'

I stopped sobbing long enough to say, 'No way,' and then I sobbed some more.

Alice sat patiently rubbing my arm until I was finished sobbing.

'Are you crying because you're afraid I'm going to get better than you at Home Ec?' she said at last.

I smiled. Trust Alice to be able to make

me smile even when it was the last thing I felt like doing.

'Well?' she said.

Suddenly I didn't know how to tell her the truth. The truth was just too bad.

So I told more lies.

'I've been getting these cramps in my stomach,' I said. 'They really hurt, but they only last for a minute or two. Then I'm fine again. I was crying just now, because the cramps were really bad. But they've stopped now. I feel better already.'

I tried to smile, but knew I wasn't doing a very good job.

Alice looked a bit doubtful.

'That sounds kind of serious,' she said. 'Have you been to a doctor or something?'

I shook my head.

'There's no need. Mum looked it up on the internet. I'll be fine again soon.'

(If I really had stomach cramps so bad that they made me cry, Mum would drag me to hospital, and keep me there until I was cured.)

Alice didn't really look convinced, but she didn't say anything for a minute.

Then she said suddenly, 'Oh, I nearly forgot to tell you. I met your friend Marcus at school yesterday. I always thought he was a bit of a messer, but he seemed really nice. He even wanted to come over to see you. I thought that was kind of sweet, but I didn't think your mum would be cool with that, so I told him it might not be a good idea.'

Alice was so busy telling her story that she didn't notice that tears were rolling down my cheeks again.

'So he seemed really disappointed,' she continued. 'And he said he can't wait to see you on Monday. He said to be sure to tell you that. He said …'

She looked at me and stopped talking.

'Hey, Meg. What is it? Is it another cramp? Please won't you let me call your mum?'

I didn't answer, and then she slapped herself on the forehead.

'I'm being totally dumb,' she said. 'You're not crying because of stomach cramps, are you? You've been worried about something for days. There's something else going on, isn't there?'

I was too tired to keep pretending, so I just nodded my head.

'Tell me what's going on,' said Alice.

Now I shook my head.

'I can't. It's too bad.'

Alice folded her arms, and looked at me seriously.

'Sit up properly, Megan,' she said. 'And

wipe your eyes.'

She seemed so determined that I decided it was best to do as she asked. So I sat up and wiped my eyes.

'Now fix your pillows, and make yourself comfortable.'

Once again I did as she said.

'Now,' she said sternly. 'There is *nothing* in the world that is so bad that you can't tell your best friend about it. So start talking.'

And so I started to talk.

Chapter twenty-six

'It's Marcus,' I began slowly. 'He sits next to me in class every single day. Well, every day that he comes to school, I mean, because lots of days he doesn't bother. And sometimes he's really nice, and funny. And sometimes, well, sometimes he's not. Sometimes he acts like he hates me.'

Alice interrupted.

'So if he hates you, why does he sit next to you?'

I shrugged.

'I don't really know. He just sat beside me on the first day, and now he still does. No one else really talks to him. All the other boys are afraid of him. And the girls are too.'

'What about you?' Alice's voice was gentle.

'A lot of the time I'm afraid of him too.'

We were both quiet for a minute. Then Alice stood up.

'That's not *toooooo* bad,' she said. 'I think we can fix this.'

I shook my head impatiently.

'But that's not the problem. That's only the start of the problem. The real problem is much, much worse.'

Alice sat down again.

'Sorry,' she said. 'Keep talking.'

So I continued my story.

'Sometimes I feel sorry for Marcus. His dad's really mean. Marcus never has any lunch. He—'

Alice slapped her forehead again.

'So you've been giving him your lunch?'

I nodded, and she continued, 'I remember you told me once that you'd given him a sandwich, but I didn't know it happened every day. I wondered why you always seem hungry at school. I should have known your mum wouldn't let you out without a day's supply of healthy food.'

Suddenly she giggled.

'And Marcus *likes* your mum's food?'

I had to giggle too.

'I know, weird, isn't it?'

Then we both got serious again.

'Anyway, go on,' said Alice.

And so I went on.

Alice gasped when I told her about the bruises on Marcus's side.

She gasped even louder when I told her about his plan to steal the exam papers.

When I told her about my part in that plan, and how the exam papers were right underneath the mattress she was sitting on, she went pale, and didn't speak for about five minutes.

Eventually she spoke in a very shocked voice.

'Please … tell me you're joking,' she said.

I shook my head.

'I can't tell you I'm joking. Because I'm not. It's all true. I don't know why I did it. I felt sorry for Marcus, and I was afraid to say no, and I took the papers and Marcus keeps sending me horrible texts, and now I don't know what to do.'

I started to cry again, and Alice hugged me tightly. While she was hugging me she was muttering angrily.

'What a *stupid* idea. Did he think he could steal papers for every exam he ever has to do? Did he think that in six year's time he'd be able to persuade you to hijack the van that brings the Leaving Cert papers so he could get a look at those too? Did he think no one would be suspicious when he doesn't do a stroke of work for months and then gets all 'A's in his exams?'

She was right, of course. They were the questions I should have asked Marcus. But I didn't. I was too afraid. Or too stupid.

I wiped my eyes again.

'What am I going to do?' I asked. 'If I give Marcus the papers, and he gets all 'A's the teachers will know something's wrong. They'll start asking questions. And they might find out that I'm the one who took them.'

I hesitated as I tried to work out the other option. Then I continued.

'And if I *don't* give Marcus the papers he'll

… I don't know what he'll do to me, but it won't be nice. And then he'll fail his exams and his dad will … well, I don't know what he'll do, but I bet that won't be nice either.'

Alice was very quiet for a very long time – so long that I began to worry about her. Had I managed to shock her so much that she didn't like me any more?

After all we had been through together, was our friendship over?

I would have cried again, but it felt like I'd run out of tears.

'I have to go in a few minutes,' Alice said eventually. 'Dad's taking me to see my granny in Portlaoise. So I won't be back until really late. But you just stay here in bed – out of trouble. Don't answer any of Marcus's messages. Don't do anything. I'll think about this all night, and I'll call over tomorrow. Just try not to worry. We'll think of a way out of this. I promise.'

Alice sounded so sure, that I began to feel better, but when she stood up to go, I didn't feel so brave any more. Then I heard a faint miaowing at the window. Alice went over and pulled back the curtain.

'It's Domino!' she said, like there were a hundred cats out there, and it could have been any one of them.

She opened the window, and Domino scrambled on to the windowsill inside. She sat there, miaowing softly.

'She can't get down,' I said. 'Will you bring her over to me?'

I'd forgotten how much Alice doesn't like cats, but then she showed me what a good friend she is. With her hand held as far away from her body as possible, she grasped Domino around the middle. Then holding her like she was a bomb that could explode at any second, she tip-toed across the room, and dropped her onto my bed. Domino immediately snuggled under the covers where it was warm.

'Thanks, Alice,' I said.

'That's OK,' she said, rubbing her hands on her jumper.

Then she hugged me one more time, and went away.

Chapter twenty-seven

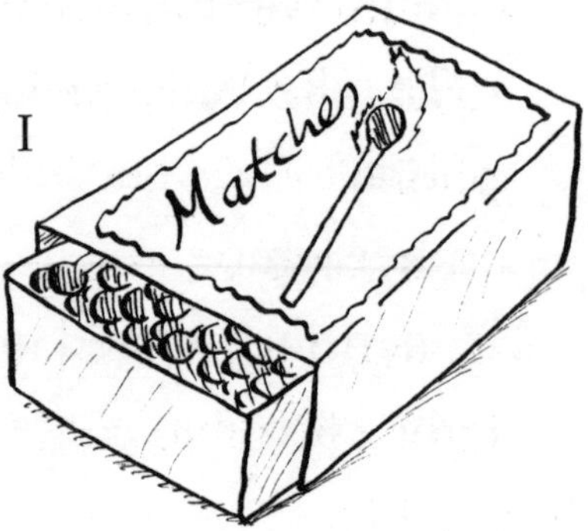

The next morning I still felt sick.

'I think it's time to call the doctor,' said Mum when she came in to see me.

'No,' I said quickly.

What was the point in seeing a doctor? No doctor could cure what was wrong with me.

Mum sighed.

'I just don't know, Megan,' she said. 'I've never seen you like this.'

That's because I've never been like this, I felt like saying, but didn't.

Instead I smiled the best smile I could manage, and said,

'I'll be better soon. I'm sure of it.'

Mum went off to make me some tea and toast, and I reached under my bed for my phone.

As well as messages from Louise and Grace, there was another one from Marcus. I got a horrible cold feeling all over when I read it.

If u don't bring the papers tomorrow U R so dead

I switched off my phone without replying, like Alice had told me to.

Then I opened my bedroom window and let Domino in. She licked my fingers with her rough tongue, and then she snuggled under my covers, and I lay back and closed my eyes.

Maybe the best thing would be to stay cuddled up in bed forever. Things would be much easier that way.

*   *   *

I was still in bed when Alice called over at lunch-time. She looked pale and tired.

'I didn't sleep very much last night,' she said.

I tried to smile.

'The first three nights are the hardest.'

She hugged me.

'Poor Megan,' she said. 'You're always so kind. You only got into all this trouble because you felt sorry for Marcus, and …'

She hesitated.

'And what?' I asked.

'Well, let's just say that I had a very interesting morning.'

'What do you mean?' I asked.

Alice sat down on my bed.

'I got up real early, and I called over to Louise's house.'

I felt a sudden spark of jealousy. I was upset and frightened, and yet Alice had got up early so she could hang out with Louise.

That didn't seem fair.

Didn't she care about me any more?

Alice didn't notice my sulky face.

'Louise's brother, Colin, was there,' she said.

I *so* didn't care about Louise's brother. He's much older than us, and spends all his time talking about football.

I put on an even sulkier face, but still Alice didn't notice.

'Colin is friends with one of Marcus's friends,' continued Alice.

At last I could see where this conversation was going. I stopped sulking and started to listen properly.

'So I decided to ask him a few things about Marcus.'

'But—', I began.

'Don't worry, I didn't mention you. I just said there was this real bad boy called Marcus in our year, and then Colin started to talk about him. It turned out he had *lots* to say.'

Now I was really listening.

'Like what?'

'Well, his mum really *is* dead, but that's about the only true thing we knew about him.'

I didn't know what she was trying to say.

'I don't understand,' I said.

'Well, Colin said that Marcus's dad is really nice. He does all kinds of good stuff for Marcus, but Marcus still gets into loads of trouble. He tells everyone that his dad is a bully, just so they'll feel sorry for him.'

'But the bruises? He didn't make them up. He *couldn't* have made them up. I saw them. They were real.'

Even thinking about the bruises on Marcus's side made me feel bad.

Alice sighed.

'I asked about them, and Colin said Marcus got those bruises in a fight with some other boys who live on his road.'

'But maybe—', I began again, but Alice interrupted me.

'Trust me. It's true. Colin saw the fight. He said it took four adults to break it up.'

I remembered the bruise Marcus had on his wrist, and the graze I'd seen on his neck one time.

It was like Alice could read my thoughts.

'Colin said Marcus is always getting into fights. In a crazy way, it's almost like he likes getting hurt.'

Suddenly I understood what she meant. I'd always felt that Marcus liked to be in trouble too.

How could anyone be as mixed up as that?

But still I found it hard to believe that Marcus was a total fraud.

'But what about the fact that his dad wouldn't buy him any school books?' I asked.

'I asked about that too. Colin just laughed. He said that Marcus's dad bought him all his school books in September, but before school even started Marcus threw them all into the river one day when he was in a temper over something.'

'But he never has any lunch,' I said. 'Or even money to buy lunch.'

Alice sighed.

'Not true either. Colin says Marcus gets money from his dad every morning, but he spends it all on cigarettes.'

I put my head in my hands.

Could this all be true?

I looked up again

'Why would Marcus do that?' I asked. 'Why would he make up all that stuff?'

'Because he's crazy?'

I shook my head.

'He's not crazy.'

Alice tried again.

'So people would feel sorry for him? So you'd feel sorry for him? I suppose it's a kind of bullying. He told you loads of lies just so you'd help him to get what he wanted.'

Suddenly it all seemed to make terrible sense.

'He was using me all the time,' I said. 'I felt so sorry for him I gave him my sandwiches.'

Alice gave a sudden giggle.

'Maybe that was punishment enough for him.'

I giggled too, and then stopped.

'I lent him my school books. I let him copy my homework. I …'

Suddenly I felt like I'd been really, really stupid. I started to cry.

'He was probably laughing behind my back all the time.'

Alice hugged me.

'You were just trying to be kind. And if he was laughing at you for being kind, then that just shows what a mean person he is. And who cares what mean people think?'

She was probably right. But I still had one problem.

'What am I supposed to do with the exam papers? I'm not afraid of what Marcus's dad will do to him, but I'm still afraid of what Marcus will do to *me* if I don't hand them over.'

'I've thought of that,' said Alice, and as

she spoke, she pulled a box of matches out of her pocket.

I gulped.

'Don't you think burning the house down is a bit extreme?'

Alice laughed.

'I'm not *that* crazy. Get up. Get dressed. Tell your mum you feel better and that we're going outside for a while.'

I did what she said, and five minutes later we were at the end of our garden, sitting in the long grass behind Rosie's old play-house. Alice was carrying the matches, and I was carrying the bundle of exam papers. Domino had followed us, and was hiding under a bush. Even she seemed to know that something big was about to happen.

Alice lit the first match. Domino gave a little squeak, and vanished into the middle of the bush. Alice held the match in the air, and then quickly blew it out. I watched as a wisp of black smoke spiralled into the cold air.

'Have you looked at the questions?' she asked.

I shook my head.

'No. I'd love to do really well in my exams, but not this way. Now light another match.'

For a minute Alice didn't move, and suddenly I understood why.

'What about you? Do you want a look before we burn these?' I asked.

Alice paused, and then shook her head.

'I *was* kind of tempted,' she said. 'I haven't worked very hard this year. And imagine what Miss Leonard would say if she had to give me an 'A' in Home Ec!'

'That would be so funny,' I said.

Alice shook her head sadly.

'But that would be cheating, and I hate

cheats. Anyway, if I did really well at Christmas, Mum and Dad would expect me always to do well, and I don't suppose you plan to steal any more papers any time soon?'

'No way,' I said quickly. 'I am never, *ever* doing anything like this again.'

Alice took out another match, and lit it. Once again she blew it out.

'I've just had the coolest idea,' she said.

'What?' I said. 'Have you figured out a way to turn the clock back, so I would never have stolen these stupid papers? Can we all go back to November, and then we'll all live happily ever after?'

'No. But it's still a cool idea. How about we find some other old exam papers, and give them to Marcus telling him they're the right ones? He'll study for ages, but he'll be studying all the wrong stuff, and he'll fail everything. Wouldn't that be so cool?'

I had to smile. Only Alice could come up with a crazy idea like that. She was right though, it would be cool. And it would serve Marcus right for all the lies he'd told me. But sadly I shook my head.

'It's a good idea, but I don't want to do it. Marcus is going to be mad enough when we don't give him these. I totally don't want to make him any madder than necessary.'

Alice sighed.

'I suppose you're right. Now here goes!'

She lit a third match. I scrunched up the exam papers and put them on the grass. Alice lit one corner of the first paper, and we watched as the whole pile blackened and burned until there was nothing left except a handful of smoking ashes.

'That's that,' said Alice. 'Now let's go back inside to figure out what we're going to say to Marcus.'

Chapter twenty-eight

Next morning Alice called for me to walk me to school. She's really not big and tall enough to be a bodyguard, but I felt safe with her beside me.

Marcus was waiting outside the school gate. From a distance he didn't look scary. He just looked like an ordinary boy who was trying to look tough.

He came over as soon as he saw me.

'Hey, Megan,' he said. 'We need to talk.'

'So talk.' I was trying to sound tough and brave, but I had a feeling that my voice was shaky.

'But it's a secret,' Marcus said looking at Alice. 'We need to talk about the …'

He stopped, so I finished his sentence for him.

' … exam papers?'

Marcus didn't answer.

'It's OK,' I said, trying not to look terrified. 'You can talk in front of Alice. She's my friend. I tell her everything.'

Suddenly Marcus looked tough again.

'Whatever. I don't care if she knows or not. The exams start tomorrow. So I need to get studying. Now hand over the papers.'

'No,' I said.

Suddenly Marcus clutched his side where the bruises were.

'Megan, stop fooling around. I have to have those papers,' he said. 'If I don't do well in my exams, my dad will—'

'Your dad will what?' asked Alice, joining in the conversation for the first time.

Marcus looked at her coldly.

'If I don't do well in my exams, my dad will beat me.'

He pulled up his shirt to show the bruises on his side, which were now a totally gross shade of greeny-yellow.

I gasped. I didn't care how he got those bruises – they still looked scary. Alice didn't look impressed though.

'We know all about you,' she said. 'We know you got those bruises in a fight. We know your dad's really nice. We know there's only one bully in your family, and that's *you*.'

Marcus went pale. He looked like Alice

had punched him in the face. Then, after a few seconds, he recovered.

'So I told a few lies,' he said. 'Get over it. Now, I still want those papers. And I'm getting impatient. So hand them over.'

'I can't,' I said.

Now Marcus looked really tough.

'Quit messing around, Megan,' he said. 'Hand over the papers.'

'I can't.'

Marcus folded his arms and stepped towards me.

'Why?'

Alice answered for me, which was just as well, as I was starting to shake. This whole scene was much too scary for me.

'Megan can't hand over the papers, because they had a bit of an accident over the weekend.'

Marcus narrowed his eyes.

'What kind of an accident?'

Alice smiled.

'The burning kind of an accident. They accidentally got burned into tiny black ashes.'

Marcus looked at me.

'Is she telling the truth?' he asked.

I didn't trust myself to speak, so I just nodded.

'I bet it wasn't an accident,' said Marcus.

Alice shrugged.

'So what? Accident or not. They're gone now, and there's nothing anyone can do about it.'

For a very long time, no one said anything. I put my hands into my pockets because they were shaking so much.

Then Marcus spoke again. He stared at me like he really hated me.

'I can tell on you, Megan,' he said. 'I never

went into the office. I never touched the exam papers. You're the only one who did something wrong.'

I gulped. Even though Alice had warned me to expect this, I was still terrified.

Marcus looked like he was enjoying himself now.

'No one will ever know I had anything to do with it.'

'But what about the fight?' I protested. 'You started a fight in the corridor.'

Marcus shrugged.

'So what? A fight's no big deal. I'm in a fight almost every day, so it's nothing special. When Mrs Kingston hears what you did, she'll forget all about my little fight. You're the one who did the really bad thing. You're the one who'll be in big, *big* trouble.'

Alice stepped forward. At first I was really

impressed at how brave she was being, but then I realised that she was enjoying herself too.

'Megan took the papers, she admits that,' she said. 'But what if she can prove that you bullied her into doing it?'

Marcus smiled an evil smile.

'But she can't, can she? She can't prove anything.'

Alice didn't answer. Instead she reached into her school-bag and pulled out a sheet of paper. She handed the paper to Marcus.

'Here,' she said. 'Read this.'

I didn't have to see the paper. I knew what was on it. All the words were written in Alice's best hand-writing, carefully copied from the screen of my mobile phone.

B at skool on Monday. Or else….

Don't forget.

If you don't bring what I want to skool on Monday I am in a lot of trouble ......

...... but not as much trouble as you.

If u don't bring the papers U R so dead

Alice was smiling. 'Look familiar?' she asked.

Marcus made an ugly face, and then tore the page into tiny little pieces.

Alice kept smiling.

'Oops,' she said. 'You seem to have accidentally torn up the evidence. But don't worry. We've made lots of copies. Megan has one. I have two more. I even gave one to my dad. He thinks I'm writing a play about bullying. And of course, Megan's phone is safe at home. Just in case anyone wants to see the original messages.'

Now Marcus didn't look tough any more.

He just looked kind of defeated. For one second, I almost felt sorry for him. Then I remembered all the lies he'd told me, and I didn't feel sorry any more. I just felt glad that I had Alice beside me to sort him out.

Marcus was starting to walk away from the school. Alice followed him, and because I couldn't think of anything else to do, I followed them both.

'If you threaten Megan – if you even think of threatening Megan,' she said. 'I'm going to Mrs Kingston. I'm going to tell her everything.'

Marcus didn't answer. He just walked away. As he walked a gust of wind blew his hair, and I could see the purple patch, faded now, half-hidden by the rest of his hair. It looked kind of pathetic. Just like him.

Chapter twenty-nine

Marcus didn't show up in class that day. Or for the rest of the week.

All the rest of us first years did our Christmas exams. Some of them were really hard. I'm not sure how well I did, but at least I didn't cheat, and that made me feel sort of good. (But maybe I'll change my mind in January, when my report arrives.)

When the exams were over, we still had a week of school left before the Christmas holidays. On the Monday, I went in to my first class. I was glad to see that Marcus wasn't there. None of the teachers mentioned him – it was almost like he'd vanished without trace – like he'd never been there at all.

After Geography, Mr Spillane asked me to help him to carry some books to the staff room. On the way, I nearly asked him about Marcus, but I stopped myself. It wasn't like I missed him or anything.

I was glad he wasn't there.

Life was easier when Marcus wasn't around.

I just kind of wondered what had happened to him.

* * *

At lunchtime, Alice was all excited when she got to the lunch-room. She was practically dragging Louise behind her.

'Tell Megan what you told me,' she prompted.

Louise fixed her school jumper where Alice had been pulling it.

'OK, OK,' she said. 'I'll tell her, but I don't see what the big deal is.'

Alice shook her head impatiently.

'It's not a big deal,' she said. 'But tell her anyway.'

Louise sighed.

'You're very bossy sometimes, you know, Alice.'

Alice grinned.

'I know. It's one of the things I'm most proud about. Now stop changing the subject, and tell Megan what you told me this morning.'

Louise sighed again.

'It's about Marcus,' she began.

'What about Marcus?' I asked weakly.

'His dad discovered about all the fights he's been involved in, and all the trouble that he's been in at school. So he's decided to send him away to boarding school in Dublin.'

'Boarding school?' I repeated.

Louise nodded.

'Yes. He's going to start his new school in January, and he's not coming back here any more. The lucky thing didn't even have to do his exams. That's not fair, is it?'

I didn't answer. I found myself repeating Marcus's words to myself.

Lots of things aren't fair.

Even though I knew he'd been telling lies about his father being a bully, I still couldn't help feeling sorry for Marcus.

How would he get on at boarding school?

Would he make any friends?

Or would he be sad and lonely?

And why did that make me feel so sad?

I noticed that Louise was staring at me.

'Hey, Megan, you and Marcus were friends, weren't you?' she said. 'Is that what this is all about?'

I looked at Alice.

She shrugged, and I knew that what happened between Marcus and me was going to remain a secret.

I shrugged too.

'Marcus and I just sat together in class sometimes. We weren't really friends.'

Louise nodded, then she turned to Alice, 'Can I go now? I've got to practice for tomorrow's carol service.'

Alice nodded, and Louise ran off.

I sat down and opened my lunch-box.

'Yum,' I said, holding the box towards Alice. 'Would you like one of my vegetable sandwiches?'

Alice shook her head.

'I'll pass this time, but thanks anyway.

Marcus would have eaten them. Pity he's not here.'

I didn't answer. Even though I was afraid of Marcus, and even though he'd bullied me into doing the worst thing I'd ever done, part of me agreed with Alice.

It *was* a pity Marcus wasn't here.

Chapter thirty

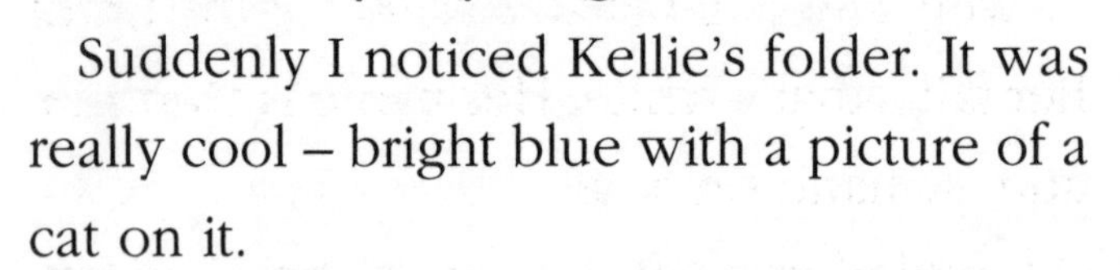

On the way back to class after lunch, I found myself walking along beside Kellie. She smiled at me, and I smiled back. Then we both got embarrassed, and didn't say anything else.

Suddenly I noticed Kellie's folder. It was really cool – bright blue with a picture of a cat on it.

'Do you like cats?' I asked. It wasn't a very smart question, because any fool could see she liked cats – she had pictures of them on all her books and folders. Kellie didn't seem to mind though. She stopped walking and looked at the picture on her folder.

'I totally love them,' she said. 'The thing I want most in the world is a cat of my own, but I can't get one. My dad's allergic, and starts sneezing if there's a cat anywhere within a hundred metres.'

'You poor thing,' I said. 'I have a cat, though. Well, she's only a kitten. She's really sweet.'

Kellie gave a big, long sigh.

'You are so, so lucky,' she said. 'What's she like?'

'Well, she's all black, except for the tip of her tail – that's white. Her name is Domino, and … hang on a sec.'

I pulled my phone out of my pocket, switched it on and held it out for Kellie to see.

'That's her. My friend Alice took this picture and sent it to me. Isn't she lovely?'

Kellie sighed again.

'I think she's the sweetest thing I've ever seen.'

Just then our teacher came along the corridor.

'Hurry up into class, girls,' she said. 'And Megan switch that phone off at once.'

Kellie went into the classroom and sat down in her usual place, and I went and sat in mine.

* * *

When I got to school the next morning, Kellie was sitting at a desk at the back of the classroom. She was chatting to two of her friends who were sitting in front of her. For a minute or two I stared at the empty seat beside Kellie.

What if she was saving it for someone?

What if she didn't want me anywhere near her?

What if …?

There were so many 'what ifs', but I knew it was time for me to brave.

I took a deep breath.

I walked across the classroom, trying not to think that everyone was staring at me.

I stood next to Kellie. She looked up and smiled.

'Hi, Megan,' she said.

'Hi,' I said.

A few seconds passed.

Then I took another deep breath.

'Could I ... I mean is that seat ...... can I ......'

I could feel my face go redder with each stupid word that came out of my mouth. Kellie was going to think that I was a total loser, and I couldn't really blame her.

I took one step backwards, and then Kellie smiled again.

'Why don't you sit here, Megan?' she said, moving her books to make room for me.

'Thanks, Kellie,' I said.

'How's Domino?' she asked as soon as I was settled in my seat.

'Great,' I replied. 'Last night she did this really funny thing.'

And when I told Kellie about what Domino had done, she laughed like she really thought it was funny. And we chatted until the teacher came in and we had to do loads of totally boring work.

* * *

Next day I got to class early. When Kellie arrived she sat next to me, like it was the most natural thing in the world.

We chatted while we were waiting for the teacher to arrive. I told her about Domino's latest tricks, and she told me about the basketball club she hoped to join after Christmas. I said she could come over after school some day and see Domino, and she said she'd like that.

Then there was a silence.

'I need to say something to you,' Kellie said after a while.

So this was it.

Did she want to tell me she didn't want to sit next to me anymore?

Had she just sat there out of kindness?

At last she spoke.

'I often wanted to sit next to you before,' she said.

'And why didn't you?' I asked. 'I'd have loved that.'

Kellie looked a bit embarrassed.

'I didn't like to because of Marcus. He was always there. I didn't want to get in the way. It looked like … it looked like there was something going on between you.'

She was right. There *was* something going on between Marcus and me. But it wasn't the way Kellie thought.

Before I could speak, she continued.

'Where is Marcus anyway? He hasn't been here for ages.'

'He's going to a new school. He's not coming back here any more.'

'And do you mind?'

How could I answer that?

Marcus is nice?

Marcus is funny?

Marcus is scary?

'It's kind of complicated,' I said in the end.

'That's OK,' she said. 'You don't have to tell me if you don't want.'

I smiled.

'Thanks. Maybe I'll tell you some other time, OK?'

And when Kellie smiled back at me, I thought maybe everything was going to turn out fine after all.

Chapter thirty-one

After school that day, Mum asked me to go to the shop to buy some vegetables for the tea.

'And take my basket,' she said. 'I don't want any child of mine to be seen carrying shopping in a plastic bag.'

'But, Mum!' I protested. 'I'll look stupid. I'll look like Little Red Riding Hood.'

Mum shook her head impatiently.

'Well, isn't that better than looking like someone who doesn't care for the environment?'

I wasn't sure about that, but I knew there was no point in arguing. I grumpily took the basket she was handing me, and went out the door.

'You'll be sorry if I meet the big bad wolf,' I said, but Mum only laughed.

Domino was playing in the garden outside, and she tried to follow me.

'No, Domino,' I said. 'Go home. You can't walk all the way to the shop.'

Domino ignored me and kept following me. Then I had an idea. I picked her up and put her into the basket. She looked totally cute, with her little black face peeping over the top, as we set off for the shop.

When I got to the corner of our road, I jumped when a figure stepped out from behind a tree.

I jumped even more when I saw that it was Marcus.

'I've been waiting for you,' he said.

I gulped and stepped backwards. It had been easy to be brave when Alice was with me, but now I realised that I was terrified.

Was he going to say that it was my fault he was being sent away to boarding school?

Domino gave a small miaow.

Why couldn't she be a tiger, who would scare Marcus away?

What use was a tiny, furry kitten?

What could she do?

Lick him to death?

Marcus reached towards the basket, but I pulled it away from him. He could pick on me if he liked, but there was *no* way I was going to let him harm my kitten.

Marcus gave me a hurt look.

'I just wanted to stroke her,' he said.

I went red.

'She's very shy,' I said. 'She's afraid of strangers.'

I went to walk past him, but he caught my arm to stop me.

'Wait,' he said. 'I need to talk to you.'

I looked around. Besides us, the street was empty. There was no one to save me. I tried to look brave, as I said, 'So talk.'

'I … I … I wanted to say sorry,' he began. 'I shouldn't have told you all those lies about my dad. I shouldn't have made you steal those papers. I shouldn't have bullied you.'

'That's OK,' I said, because I couldn't think of anything else to say.

'It's not OK,' said Marcus so fiercely that I stepped back again. 'It's not one bit OK. You're the only one who was nice to me. You helped me with my work, you gave me your lunches, and all I did was bully you. It is *so* not OK.'

I smiled at him.

'Really, it's OK. It's all over now. It's—'

Marcus interrupted me.

'I've been really mixed up lately. It's almost like I couldn't help myself. Since my mum died ... I don't know ... nothing seemed right any more.'

He put his head down and his hair fell over his forehead. I stood there, wondering what I should do.

Suddenly he put his head up and tried to smile.

'Anyway, I think things are better now. Dad and I had a long talk. A proper talk – the first one we've had in ages. I think we're going to be able to work things out.'

I smiled back at him.

'I'm glad, Marcus,' I said. 'I really am.'

'And I'm off to boarding school after

Christmas,' he said.

'And are you OK with that?'

He shrugged.

'I think it's for the best. I made a bad start here. I'd like an opportunity to start again.'

I had a sudden thought.

'A girl I know, Melissa, she's in boarding school in Dublin. Maybe you'll be in her school.'

He shook his head.

'I'm going to an all-boys school, so I don't think so.'

Maybe it was for the best. His life was hard enough already. He *so* didn't need Melissa in it making things even worse.

'I need to go,' he said. 'Dad's taking me to buy my new school uniform.'

I giggled.

'And are you going to wear it this time?'

He shrugged.

'Maybe.'

I put on a cross face, and he sighed.

'OK, I'll wear it, but only because you asked me to.'

Then he gave me a hug. I was really surprised, but before I could say anything, he walked away. Just as he was turning the corner, he looked back.

'Megan,' he called.

'What?'

'Will you text me at boarding school?'

I nodded.

'Sure I will. I promise.'

Then Domino and I continued our journey to the shop.

* * *

When I got back home, Mum met me in the hall.

'Well then,' she said. 'Did you meet the

big bad wolf?'

I just laughed.

'You wouldn't believe me if I told you.'

Mum shook her head.

'Teenagers,' she sighed. 'I'll never understand you.'

Chapter thirty-two

Friday was the day we got our Christmas holidays. Last class was Home Ec as usual. We were baking Christmas logs. It was Alice's turn to cook, so Grace and I were looking forward to an entertaining afternoon.

Miss Leonard had asked every person who was cooking to bring in a piece of plastic holly to decorate their finished log.

She arrived at our table just as Alice was putting out her ingredients.

'I don't

suppose you remembered your holly?' she said to Alice.

Alice beamed at her.

'Oh, I did, Miss,' she said. 'But I didn't stop at holly. I brought loads of great stuff. My log is going to be *sooooo* cool. I bet it'll be the best log you've ever seen.'

As she spoke she reached into her school-bag and pulled out a huge bag filled with plastic santas and elves and angels. She was so busy lining them up on her table in a crazy Christmas procession, that she didn't notice the look of horror on Miss Leonard's face.

'This is the best one,' Alice said, pulling out a huge, ugly reindeer and placing it on the table. She pressed one of its antlers, and it began to play '*Grandma got run over by a reindeer*' really loudly. Everyone stopped talking and began to laugh. Miss Leonard made a funny shape with her mouth, like she'd sucked a lemon or something.

'My dear Alice,' she said. 'You seem to forget that this is Home Economics, not a class in modern sculpture.'

Alice shrugged.

'I just thought I'd try to brighten up my log. That's all.'

Miss Leonard did her sucky-lemon face again.

'Concentrate on not making your log poisonous, and you'll be doing very well,' she said.

Then she moved on to the next group.

* * *

At the end of the class, Alice stepped back to admire her log. All the other logs were pretty, log-shaped cakes. Alice's looked like something that had been trampled by a herd of very big and very angry elephants.

She didn't seem to mind too much.

'Lucky I brought these extra decorations,' she said.

Grace and I helped her until the cake was completely hidden under a pile of ugly plastic creatures.

Just then Miss Leonard came along.

'Hmm, Alice,' she said. 'Are you sure you wouldn't prefer to join the art class? It's not to late to change, you know.'

Alice smiled.

'No thanks, Miss. I *love* Home Ec. In fact it's my very favourite subject. I'm going to do it all the way to Leaving Cert.'

Miss Leonard looked like she was going to faint at the thought of having to teach Alice for all those years.

Grace and I laughed. The future was starting to look very bright.

*   *   *

As soon as the class was over, Alice and I set off for home. When we got to the school gate, Alice stopped suddenly.

'Why am I bringing all these books home?' she said. 'It's not like I'm going to study over the holidays or anything stupid like that. Here, hold this, while I go back to my locker.'

She handed me the Christmas log, which looked more like a project in modern art.

'Thanks a million,' I said.

Alice seemed to be gone for ages, and everyone who went past me stared at me and laughed, so I was very happy when she came back.

I handed the Christmas log to Alice. There was no way I was walking all the way home with that in my hands.

'What will I do about this?' she asked. 'Will I give it to Dad or to Mum?'

Who do you love the least? I thought.

Once again Alice managed to read my mind. She looked closely at the log.

'It's not very nice is it?'

I didn't answer.

Suddenly Alice gave a huge smile.

'Back in a sec,' she said, and she raced back into school, leaving a trail of plastic elves behind her.

When she came back, the log was gone.

'What did you do with it?'

Alice smiled.

'I gave it to Miss Leonard,' she said. 'I told her it was her Christmas present.'

I giggled.

'What did she say?'

Alice giggled too.

'She said I'm the most interesting student

she's ever taught.'

Just then Grace and Louise came along. Grace was all excited, because the next day was going to be her thirteenth birthday. She is totally spoiled, so she was bringing loads of us ice-skating and then on to a real fancy restaurant for dinner.

'Guess what? My two cousins can't come tomorrow after all,' said Grace as she joined us.

'So you've got two spare tickets for the skating?' said Alice.

Grace wrinkled her nose.

'Not exactly. My mum met Melissa's mum in the shopping centre yesterday, and Mum invited Melissa to my party.'

The rest of us groaned, until Alice waved her hand to stop us.

'Let's just be nice to Melissa, and we can call it our good deed for Christmas.'

Louise giggled.

'So what are you going to do with the other ticket?' she asked Grace.

Grace shrugged.

'I don't know. I've already invited all of my friends. Any of you want to ask someone?'

Louise and Alice shook their heads, but I suddenly had an idea.

'There's this girl in my class, Kellie. She's really nice. I think you'd all like her. I could ask her, if you like.'

'Sure,' said Grace.

I grinned.

'Thanks. I'll text her as soon as I get home.'

By then we were at the turn for Grace and Louise's houses, so we all hugged and they went off.

When we got to my house, Alice and I stopped.

'You know what Miss Leonard said, about me being interesting?' she asked.

I nodded.

'Do you think that means she likes me?' she asked.

I was fairly sure it meant the opposite, but couldn't think of a nice way of saying so.

Alice looked at me closely, and I felt like she was reading my mind again.

Then she laughed.

'It's the Christmas holidays, so who cares what Miss Leonard thinks?'

'I've been thinking too,' I said suddenly. 'I never thanked you properly for helping me to stand up to Marcus that time. So thank you.'

As I spoke I gave her a quick hug.

Alice shrugged.

'It's nothing,' she said. 'That's what friends do for each other.'

But her face had gone slightly red, and I knew she was pleased.

'I'm going to change out of my uniform,' she said. 'Call for you later?'

I nodded.

'Sure.'

I went in my gate and up the path.

Domino was waiting for me, all curled up on one of Mum's plant pots. I picked her up and cuddled her.

'I am so, so happy,' I said suddenly.

Domino didn't reply, but I think she understood.

South Dublin Libraries
www.southdublinlibraries.ie

www.obrien.ie